ABOUT THE AUTHOR

ZOYA PIRZAD is a renowned Iranian–Armenian writer and novelist. Her debut novel, the international bestseller *Things We Left Unsaid* (*Cheragh-ha ra man khamush mikonam*) published by Oneworld in 2012, won numerous awards, including the prestigious Hooshang Golshiri award for Best Novel of the Year, and has been translated into several languages. Her most recent collection of stories, *The Bitter Taste of Persimmon*, won the prize for Best Foreign Book of 2009 in France. She grew up in Abadan, Iran, and now lives in Yerevan, Armenia.

THE SPACE BETWEEN US

Zoya Pirzad

Translated by
Amy Motlagh

ONEWORLD

A Oneworld Book

First published in English in North America, Great Britain
& Australia by Oneworld Publications, 2014

First published by Nashr-e-Markaz as *Yek Ruz Mande be Eid Pak*, 1998

English translation rights arranged through
agreement with Zulma, France

Copyright © Nashr-e-Markaz Publishing Company, Tehran, Iran, 1998

Translation copyright © Amy Motlagh, 2014

The moral right of Zoya Pirzad to be identified as the
Author of this work has been asserted by her in accordance
with the Copyright, Designs and Patents Act 1988

Hardback ISBN 978-1-85168-997-2
ebook ISBN 978-1-78074-237-3

Printed and bound by CPI Group (UK) Ltd, Croydon, CR0 4YY

The characters and events in this novel are fictitious.
Any similarity to real persons, living or dead, is
coincidental and not intended by the author.

Oneworld Publications
10 Bloomsbury Street
London WC1B 3SR
England

CONTENTS

THE SPACE
BETWEEN US

PART I

sour cherry stones

MY CHILDHOOD HOME was right next door to both the church and the school. Its courtyard, like all the courtyards in our small coastal town, was full of orange trees. In front of the veranda on the ground floor, there was a small rectangular flower bed where my father planted flowers in the spring and summer, and which overran with rainwater in the fall and winter. The ground floor of the house was an apartment with large, high-ceilinged rooms and wooden columns: in the mornings it was flooded with light from the courtyard, but in the afternoons it was very dark.

No one lived on the ground floor. Effat, who came once a week to do the laundry, stored her tubs and soap there, and when the weather was rainy she would hang the washing from clothes lines strung between the columns. In there, Mother hid away items that she couldn't bear to throw away yet: my cradle; my scooter; the bicycle she'd ridden in her own childhood; a wardrobe with two mirrored doors that she said was the only thing left from her mother's dowry. My father's hunting gear was down there in one of the rooms, too. Every time my father asked, "Why don't you rent the downstairs?" my mother would shrug and say, "I don't have the patience for tenants."

Until I started school, I filled my mornings playing downstairs in the abandoned rooms among the drying laundry and things that had no use. In the afternoons, I played upstairs in the sitting room with my toys, or flipped through newspapers and magazines and blackened the holes in the letters with a pencil. My bedroom was next to the sitting room, and before I fell asleep I would listen to the sounds coming from there. On the evenings when we didn't have guests, the soft shooshing static of Radio Armenia could be heard, or the sound of my parents' bickering.

To reach the second floor, we used the narrow wooden stairs that began in the courtyard and led to the upper balcony, which was larger and wider than the veranda below. The windows of the upper floor on one side opened onto the balcony and on the other overlooked the courtyard of the school and church.

The church was a rectangular gray stone building with six high, narrow windows that I had never seen open. My grandmother said that the church and school had been built by the first Armenian immigrants who settled in our seaside town.

The school had two floors and a white stone facade. In the middle of every other stone a five-petaled flower was carved. When I was very small, I would pull a chair over to the window, sit with my legs crossed, and watch the comings and goings at the school and church. I could never follow the games the children played during recess: my eyes were fixed on the five-petaled flowers. I thought that when I went to school, I wouldn't run around excitedly during recess, but rather, handkerchief in hand, I'd clean out the moss that gathered between the petals. I imagined that when I grew up, I'd be taller, and able to reach even the highest flowers on the lower floor. For the flowers on the upper floor, though, I was stumped. One afternoon when we were in second grade, Tahereh and I were playing in the schoolyard, and she said, "I know! We'll build a very tall ladder. Then we can reach all the flowers." Then, as if she read my mind, she added, "If you're scared, you can stay down here and hold the ladder. I'll go up."

The courtyard of the school and church was the only place where Tahereh and I could play together after school. Tahereh never came to our house, maybe because she knew that my father wouldn't like it. The room that Tahereh shared with her mother and father, on the ground floor of the school, was small and didn't have enough space for us to play. Also, if my father knew that I'd gone to the janitor's quarters, he would have thrown a fit, and my mother and I would have been forced to listen to a long and repetitive lecture about class and religion and the differences between people.

Behind the church there was a graveyard. There was no wall between the graveyard and the courtyard, maybe because there was no need for it. The principal had forbidden the students from going into the graveyard and the word of the principal was, for us, the highest and most daunting of all walls.

It had been years since anyone had been buried there. The new Armenian cemetery was a few kilometers outside the city, on the road to Tehran. Grandmother said that the last "eternal sleeper" laid to rest in the old graveyard was her childhood friend Anahid, who had caught meningitis and by the time they got her to the doctor…

Grandmother never spoke directly about death.

It was on a rainy afternoon at my grandmother's house, before I'd even started attending school, that I first heard the story of Anahid. Staring at the flames in the cast-iron heater, I imagined my grandmother's childhood friend and, although I'd never heard her described, I was positive that she must have been a thin, blond girl with a mole on one of her cheeks. For a long time I kept asking my mother and grandmother and aunt, and every other adult around me, "When I turn twelve, will I get meningitis and die?"

No one was able to persuade me otherwise.

My mother asked my father angrily, "Why is your mother always talking about that dead person in front of the child?"

My father defended his mother and as usual it turned into a fight. Meanwhile, I would hide in a corner of the house, crying over my own fated death at the age of twelve. Then one day my grandmother took me in her arms, sat me on her lap, and said, "Listen, Edmond. Anahid got meningitis because she was a girl. Boys never get meningitis."

My parents stared open-mouthed at Grandmother, but because I had finally heard what in my opinion was a convincing explanation, I was satisfied, and didn't fear my death at the age of twelve any longer.

That year I turned twelve.

Early one morning, a few days before Easter, I stood on the balcony at the top of the stairs that ran down to the courtyard and ran my hand over the banister. *No sliding down today*, I thought. It was still wet from last night's rain. I went down the stairs one by one.

From the kitchen my mother yelled, "Don't drag your satchel on the stairs!"

I slung my school bag over my shoulder, stood on the bottom step, and looked around the courtyard. The trees were in full bloom; a few more days and the town would be filled with the smell of orange blossom. I looked at the garden. It was amazing how high the snapdragons had grown since yesterday! And then suddenly…I closed my eyes and tried to make a wish.

Mother always said, "Every spring, the first ladybug that you see, close your eyes and make a wish."

But I had no other wish *except* to see the ladybug. I opened my eyes and there it was, making its way along the stalk of a snapdragon. Its red body with the black spots looked so pretty on the pale green stem! I put my finger in its path and it crawled up.

Mother said, "Once you've made a wish, let it go. By Easter, your wish will come true."

I thought to myself, *I'll just keep it with me until I make my wish.*

I shrugged my satchel onto the ground, keeping the ladybug in the palm of one hand and covering it with the other, and ran up the wooden stairs two at a time. When I reached the upstairs balcony, I crept past the kitchen, the dining room, then the sitting room, praying that neither Mother nor Father would look up.

I was sure my father would say, "Stop being a baby!"

I knew that Mother would have been happy to see the ladybug, but now wasn't the time. I was going to be late for school.

In my room, I opened one of the thirty or forty matchboxes that I'd collected and dropped the ladybug into it, whispering, "Stay here until I get back."

Just as I got to the top of the stairs, Mother came outside. "What are you doing here? The school bell already rang!"

I slid down the wet banister, grabbed my bag, and ran.

I was late.

The other pupils were already standing in line, reciting the morning prayer. "Our Father, who art in heaven…"

"…art in heaven," I recited with the other kids and thanked God that the principal's eyes were shut and he hadn't seen me come in late.

I found a place at the end of the line behind Tahereh. Tahereh's eyes were closed. Palms clasped together, head bowed, the tip of her nose touching the tops of her fingers.

"What did you find?" she whispered.

I dropped my bag on the ground, quickly crossed myself, bowed my head, and recited, "Forgive us our sins…"

I whispered back, "A ladybug."

Tahereh's eyes sparkled as she turned towards me. "Did you make a wish?"

The principal announced loudly, "Sixth grade."

Our line shuffled out towards the classroom.

As we made our way up the stairs, I wondered how she knew I'd found something. I wanted to ask, but then I changed my mind. There were now a few other children between Tahereh and me. Anyway, if I asked, she would probably just cross her eyes or pull a funny face and say, "I'm a sorcerer!"

Our first class was Armenian history. I had studied, so when the teacher called out "Edmond Lazarian," I felt confident and jumped up to stand at the front of the class.

The teacher asked, "Which Armenian king was known by the epithet 'Beloved'?"

But as soon as I opened my mouth, I forgot the

name of the teacher and the lesson and all of the Armenian kings. Instead I remembered that I hadn't made a hole in the lid of the matchbox and now the ladybug would suffocate and die.

The teacher said, "I asked, which king of Armenia was known by the epithet 'Beloved'?"

From the bench in front of me, Tahereh whispered something.

With my eyes on Tahereh's mouth and my thoughts with the ladybug, I repeated what Tahereh had said. "Sultan Hamid the Second*."

The children started snickering and the teacher shouted, "Knock it off!"

When the recess bell rang, Tahereh came over to me as though nothing had happened. "Where did you find it?"

I put my index finger in my mouth, brought it out, and shook it at the ground. Meaning, *I'm not talking to you.* Tahereh shrugged and turned around so fast that her two braids hit me in the face.

During the second recess, I leaned against the wall of the courtyard, gloomy and bored, watching the first-graders play hide and seek. Tahereh was handing out the marked dictation notebooks. I watched her out of the corner of my eye to see if she was coming towards me. I was still upset.

She came over to me and beamed. "You got an A!"

I put my finger in my mouth, pulled it out, and this time I shook it twice at the ground. *I'm* really *not talking to you.* Tahereh refused to look at me for the rest of the day and when the last bell rang, she rushed out of the classroom before anyone else.

Angry with myself and feeling ashamed, I started to collect my things. Angry because I had sulked and refused to speak with her; ashamed because I hadn't tried to meet her halfway. I tried to remember what my father always said: "All a man has is his pride." I picked up my bag, and then remembered how my mother would snort and say, "Men call their foolishness 'pride.'"

I was still trying to decide who was right as I walked out of the classroom when suddenly someone leaped in front of me. "Boo!"

I nearly jumped out of my skin.

Tahereh laughed. "Did I scare you?"

She didn't even give me a chance to reply. She stamped her foot and said, "For Christ's sake! Let's make up."

Then she put her hand on my arm and tilted her head. "Please? You're my only friend."

Being Tahereh's only friend was my dearest wish. In fact, being Tahereh's friend was the dream of every boy in the school plus the few girls who weren't jealous of her. I held out my pinky finger. Tahereh put hers out, too, and we locked them together, shook them down three times, and said together, "Peace."

Just as I was thinking how nice it was not to feel sad anymore, I remembered the ladybug. I ran.

At the bottom of the stairs I turned my head and shouted, "This afternoon in the courtyard!"

Tahereh was standing on the balcony watching me. I ran through the school gates and bumped straight into my father, who was just outside. "What's going on?"

"Nothing," I said. "Hello. Nothing."

I tried to nip past him but he grabbed my arm. "We're going to the barber."

I despaired. Now the ladybug would die for sure. I searched for an excuse. "Can I go home and come back?"

"Why? What for?"

"Just…something…I want to put my bag in my room."

My father opened the door to our courtyard, took my bag, dumped it inside, and said, "Let's go."

I couldn't bring myself to mention the ladybug. If he knew, he'd immediately go and kill it if it wasn't dead already. Then he would say, "How many times have I told you not to be such a sissy?" Then he'd blame my mother. "This is your fault. He's learning all this prissy-boy crap from you."

Mr. Reza the barber shaved my head with the number-two setting on his clippers while my father and Mr. Abraham sat on two wobbly wooden chairs and talked.

Mr. Abraham was my classmate Anush's father. She was a chubby girl with frizzy hair who was always getting in fights and called Tahereh "Daughter of the Muslim janitor!" We didn't get along either. Last week, we were playing a game of Duck-Duck-Goose in front of the church during recess when Anush picked a fight with Tahereh. When I defended Tahereh, Anush called out, "Mama's boy, mama's boy, you're in love with the Muslim janitor's daughter!" While I was still trying to decide how to respond, Tahereh marched over and slapped Anush's cheek hard. That was when Anush's nose started to bleed.

The principal and all the teachers rushed outside. One of the teachers pressed a damp handkerchief to Anush's forehead and the principal asked what had happened. Anush, sobbing and screaming, shouted that Tahereh had hit her. The principal came over to Tahereh, who clasped her hands behind her back, bent her head, and with the toe of her shoe kicked the sand in the courtyard back and forth. However much the principal and teachers demanded that she tell them why she had hit Anush, she wouldn't say a word. That day, for the first time, the principal punished Tahereh. It was such an astonishing event that everyone forgot what the original offense had been.

Now Mr. Abraham was whispering something in my father's ear. I could see them in the mirror. Suddenly I was terrified. Had Anush told her father? Was he telling my father the whole story now?

When my father chuckled softly, I let out a sigh of relief. He didn't know. Still laughing, he put a hand on Anush's father's knee. "Come on! Tell the truth."

Mr. Abraham laughed. "Would I lie to you? Besides, there was a witness."

"Who?" my father asked. Anush's father gestured with his left hand.

To the left of the barbershop, just across from the school and the church and our house, was Mrs. Grigorian's sherbet* shop. She lived in the flat above her shop and was a close friend of my grandmother's.

Mr. Reza glanced at his apprentice, who was sweeping the sidewalk in front of the barbershop, and yelled at him in Gilaki.*

My father said, "But the shop isn't open at night."

"She saw it from the upstairs window."

"What did the janitor's wife say?"

"First she cried, then she said, 'Shame on you, you're old enough to be my father.'"

"What did Mrs. Grigorian say?"

"She said, 'I spit on you! You're old enough to be my father, too!'"

My father and Mr. Abraham started to snort and laugh, slapping their knees. My father, chuckling, said, "So, Simonian is still at it…"

Mr. Reza untied the big white cape from around my neck.

My father put a bill in Mr. Reza's hand and turned to me. "You go home. Tell your mother I'll be back late tonight."

I don't know how I managed to get myself across the street. The door to our courtyard was open. I kicked my school bag out of the way, ran across the courtyard, and leaped up the wooden stairs two steps at a time. Through the open window I saw Mother and Grandmother sitting in the kitchen, but before either of them could say anything, I made it to my room.

I opened the lid of the matchbox. Then I put my head in my hands and felt the tears running down my face.

The door to my room opened, startling me. If it was my father, he would taunt me. *Real men don't cry!*

It was my mother. Mother never made fun of me for crying. She cried, too, sometimes, when the house was quiet and nobody else was around. If I put my hand on her shoulder and asked, "Why are you crying?" she would force a smile and say, "Sometimes I just feel sad."

Now she put a hand on my shoulder. "Why are you crying?"

I showed her the ladybug and she took the matchbox from my hand. "Poor thing."

This only made me cry harder. "It's my fault! If I hadn't taken it out of the garden, or if I hadn't put it in the matchbox, or if I had remembered to leave a hole in the box…"

Mother stroked my head gently. "There's no use crying over spilled milk. Everything and everyone dies eventually. Get up now, get up and go say hello to your grandmother. If you don't, we'll really have a disaster."

My grandmother was sitting at the kitchen table. As always, she sat up straight on the edge of the chair, as if she was ready to get up and go right then. A white handkerchief bordered with embroidery was tucked into the sleeve of her black dress. My sadness over the ladybug faded. I thought what a shame it was that I hadn't been here when my grandmother arrived to watch her wipe off the chair before she sat down.

Whenever my grandmother came to our house, she pulled the white handkerchief out of the sleeve of her dress, which was always black, and dusted off whatever chair she wanted to sit on. It made me think of the Indian magician I had seen a few years ago during the end-of-school-year party, who pulled colored handkerchiefs out of the sleeve of his black coat.

My father found it funny. "My mother has OCD," he'd joke. It made my mother mad, though. "So why doesn't she do it at her daughter's house then?" she'd ask.

After I greeted her, my grandmother gave her usual sigh and put a hand on my cheek. "Why does this child get thinner each time I see him?"

She eyed me as if my imminent death had just been announced. Then she cast the same mournful look over the grape leaves that were spread out on the kitchen table. "Aren't these leaves wonderful? Soft as velvet. Yesterday I took some for Shakeh, too, and she made such delicious *dolma**with them. Fine and even as a strand of pearls. I don't know if you have the patience for making *dolma*, though. If you don't want them…"

Grandmother stroked the grape leaves regretfully. My mother's lips tightened into a thin line, then she looked at me and snapped. "Don't you have any homework to do?"

In my room I closed my Persian notebook and thought about the composition I was supposed to write in Armenian. The prompt was, *What are our responsibilities to our homeland?* Each year, ever since we had started writing compositions, we had to write this essay. At first, the responsibilities were simple: we must learn our mother tongue well, we must never forget our homeland, and we must pray to God for the freedom of our homeland. But now that I was in the sixth grade, I thought that perhaps I should try to explain our responsibilities in a more complex fashion.

Like the other Armenians in our small coastal town, I had only seen Armenia on a map; old maps in textbooks or in the bulky tomes that older people kept in their homes. In Grandmother's sitting room, there was an enormous antique map of Armenia on the wall: a gift from Mrs. Grigorian.

Mrs. Grigorian was the only Armenian in our town who had seen Armenia, and what respect she derived from this distinction! She was invited to every engagement party and wedding and baptism, and a place was always set for her at the best table. When dinner was over, the guests would praise the hosts for their generosity, the young couple or the newborn was wished good luck and good health, and then Mrs. Grigorian was asked to talk about her memories of Armenia. Mrs. Grigorian, tiny and thin and blue-eyed, wearing a milky-white dress with a lace collar, would cough a few times, and wait for silence in the room. Then she'd fix her eyes on a salt shaker or a fork or a piece of bread on the table, and begin.

I knew all of Mrs. Grigorian's reminiscences by heart, and as soon as she started, I knew immediately which one she was about to tell: the story of her pilgrimage to Ejmiatsin* Cathedral that had lasted forty days, or the ritual of grape-picking in the vineyards, or the tale of her own eventful emigration from Armenia to Iran. The main features of these recollections were the same, but the details changed a little bit each time.

One night before bed, Grandmother was reading me the story of Little Red Riding Hood. She got to the part where the wolf ate Little Red Riding Hood's grandmother. This scene made me cry, and I begged, "This time, let's pretend the wolf didn't eat the grandmother."

My grandmother laughed. "But we cannot change the story."

I looked at the wolf on the cover of the book and said, "So why does Mrs. Grigorian change *her* stories then?"

Grandmother's little eyes grew wide. "'*Therefore why* does Mrs. Grigorian change her stories,' not 'so why.' Furthermore, Mrs. Grigorian's memories are not *stories*! When you grow up you'll understand! And let this be the last time I hear you call your elders liars!" She threw the book onto the bed and left the room.

This wasn't the first time Grandmother had corrected my Armenian, but I'd never seen her this angry before. I picked the book up gingerly to avoid touching the picture of the wolf, climbed off the mattress, and put the book face down under the bed. If the picture of the wolf was face up at night, I would be afraid and wouldn't sleep. I got back under the covers and wondered when I had ever called Mrs. Grigorian a liar.

I thought I might begin my composition with one of Mrs. Grigorian's stories that had a patriotic slant. However, I wanted to embellish it with a little extra sparkle. If Mrs. Grigorian could add a little something every time she told her stories, why couldn't I? Then I would finish up with a couple of long and difficult words and patriotic slogans. The Armenian literature teacher loved complicated words.

I started a few opening sentences and crossed them out. The opening sentence was always the hardest for me. I wished Tahereh were here to help me. Tahereh's Armenian composition, like the rest of her subjects, was better than everyone else's, including mine. There wasn't a child in the school that hadn't been compared unfavorably to Tahereh at some point: "Aren't you ashamed? The daughter of the Muslim janitor speaks your mother tongue better than you do!" I wondered what Tahereh would write for her composition. Our motherland wasn't her motherland, after all.

I went to the window and stood there trying to think of an opening sentence. From where I stood, I could see the trees in the graveyard, the movement of the tall weeds, and a few gravestones.

The gravestones behind the church were mostly oblong and small, with stone crosses on them, but there were some bigger graves too with elaborately carved gravestones and memorial statues. One that stood out was a rectangular cube resembling a stone bench which lay in the front courtyard under one of the church windows. There was nothing written on this stone. Not even Grandmother and Mrs. Grigorian knew why it was called the priest's grave. But on All Saints' Day, they burned incense on this nameless and unknown grave as they did on all the others.

I rarely went to the graveyard behind the church. Once I had gone with Grandmother after I had scarlet fever, because Grandmother had made a vow that if I recovered, I would circumambulate the church seven times. And I had gone a few other times after school because Tahereh insisted that playing among the graves was fun.

Playing among the graves was no fun for me. The principal's admonitions not to go there scared me, and the fetid smell and sight of all the mossy crosses made me feel a little sick. The only temptation that induced me to go along with Tahereh, after some pressure, was the statue of the merchant's wife.

This was the biggest gravestone: a lifelike statue of a woman sitting on a bench, head bowed over a book held in her hand. Grandmother said that it had been made for the headstone of an Armenian merchant's grave many years ago. The merchant had traded between Iran and Russia. When he died, his wife commissioned a stonemason to come from Russia to carve a memorial statue. On the first anniversary of the merchant's death, the statue was placed on the grave, and everyone was surprised to see that it closely resembled the merchant's wife. And a few days later, she left for Russia, in the company of the stonemason.

Time and humidity and rain had worn away most of the gravestones, but the marble statue of the merchant's wife was intact. Tahereh and I had often run our hands over the stone shawl that covered a portion of her stone hair and shoulders. The statue looked so lifelike to me that sometimes I thought I could pull up the shawl to cover the rest of her hair and bare shoulder.

I drew the heavy curtain over the window and went back to my desk. By the time I had finished copying out my composition in clean handwriting, it was late afternoon. Tahereh would be waiting for me.

My mother was rolling *dolma* in the kitchen. "I'm going to see Tahereh," I said.

When she didn't raise her head, I knew she wasn't in a good mood.

I made up an excuse. "I need to ask her something."

Now she raised her head. "What?"

I looked at the pile of lumpy, uneven *dolma* piled in the pot. "Um…I want her to correct my Armenian composition."

Mother straightened up so fast that the gold chain with the jeweled cross around her neck swung up and caught on the button of her collar. "You need the daughter of the Muslim janitor to correct your Armenian composition? You should be ashamed of yourself!"

I was used to the fact that Mother went into a bad temper after Grandmother's visits, but not to this extent. She never called Tahereh "the Muslim janitor's daughter." Maybe this time Grandmother had gone too far, or maybe it was because, on top of Grandmother's visit, Father had said he would be home late.

I ran a hand over my head. Because of my crew cut, the closely shaved skin on my head tingled and the fine little cut hairs irritated the back of my neck. I looked out of the window at the balcony and tried to come up with a better excuse. The white paint on the balcony rail was peeling off and on the windowsill the leaves of the flowers in the geranium pots were turning yellow. Mother had probably forgotten to water them again.

I remembered last winter when we had been invited to Auntie Shakeh's house.

My aunt had brought out a plate of herbs that she had grown herself in the greenhouse and set it on the table. When guests praised her skills my father had added, "But no one is as skillful as my wife. In a town where even the stones flower, my wife can dry out a tree in two days flat!"

Grandmother and Auntie, who were the slowest to smile most of the time, laughed the loudest.

There were still a lot of grape leaves and *dolma* filling on the table. Sensing that pushing the point wouldn't help, and just to say something, I asked, "Are we having *dolma* for dinner?"

Mother didn't answer. I was thinking of calling out to Tahereh from the window to say that I wasn't coming when one of the grape leaves burst in Mother's hand and the stuffing spilled onto the table. My mother clenched her fist, pounded on the table, and said, "Dammit!"

Suddenly I had an idea. "Your *dolma* are *much* better than Auntie Shakeh's."

Mother remained silent for a few moments. Then she unclenched her fists slowly. "Go," she said. "But come back soon."

As I closed the door to the house, I took a deep breath. A raindrop fell on my head. The smell of fresh bread drifted over from the bakery near our house. I thought of going to buy sweet buns. Tahereh loved sweet buns. Then I realized that if it started to rain, we wouldn't be able to play. On the other side of the street, the lights of the sherbet shop were on. Mrs. Grigorian was standing behind the counter and talking with a man and woman, each of whom had a glass of sherbet in their hands.

I didn't like any of Mrs. Grigorian's sherbets – not the sour cherry nor the orange, and not the lemon either – but I loved the sherbet machine that had three tall, thin glass urns with fine etchings of flowers and leaves. On the two outer vessels, two eagles stood with open wings, looking at one another. Above the sherbet machine, on the wall of the shop, was a large oil painting of the two peaks of Mount Ararat*: Greater Ararat and Lesser Ararat. Mrs. Grigorian had brought the painting with her from Armenia. My father, who was a member of the church and school council, said that Mrs. Grigorian had willed that the painting be left to the school when she died. Tahereh had asked me a few times, "But what about the sherbet machine?" and I had asked my father,

"But what about the sherbet machine?" but all he did was shrug.

The couple left the shop. Mrs. Grigorian's hand was moving in a circle over the counter. I knew she was wiping it with her white flowered tea towel.

Mrs. Grigorian's tea towels were all white and flowered. Large flowers or small, red or yellow or blue. Knowing the names of the flowers on the tea towel was one of the special games that Tahereh and I had made up. When I was in first grade, on the afternoon that I learned the letter "L" in Persian and I could write "tulip," I went with my father to Mrs. Grigorian's sherbet shop. My father and Mrs. Grigorian talked and I examined the colored flowers on the crumpled tea towel on the counter.

My father said, "He has been the school janitor for many years. Now that his daughter has reached school age, it would not be pleasing to the Lord to send her far away to another school because she is not Armenian. The council has agreed that the little girl can attend our school, may it please God." He was talking in the same stilted and self-important tone that he did at home whenever he practiced his speeches for the church and school meetings.

Mrs. Grigorian put a glass of sour-cherry sherbet in front of me.

"I don't like sherbet," I said. "Are the flowers on your tea towel tulips?" I said "tulip" in Persian and Mrs. Grigorian laughed. "'Tulip' in Armenian is *kakach*."* Then she turned to my father and said more seriously, "You are right. The Lord would not be pleased."

I walked through the open school gate into the courtyard. Nobody was there. I ran until I reached the priest's grave. I hoisted myself up and sat down on it. My feet didn't reach the ground but swung in the air. The wind murmured against my scalp. I ran a hand over my head and prayed that Tahereh wouldn't laugh at my ridiculously short haircut. My back was to the church. The classroom lights on the top floor of the school were all turned out, apart from in the first room on the right where an open window emitted yellow light. The principal of the school lived here. Among the row of classrooms on the lower floor, again only one light was on. This was the room where Tahereh lived with her mother and father. I focused for so long at the school building with its dark exterior and the two lit windows that it started to look like a face with a large gaping mouth and two loose teeth. At first this made me laugh, but then my head turned involuntarily and I glanced at the church behind me and became afraid. A chill crept over me from the gravestone. Why hadn't Tahereh come? I looked at the door to the janitor's room, then towards our own house. There was no one at the windows. I jumped off the gravestone and ran.

Tahereh's mother opened the wooden door. Her *chador* had fallen around her shoulders. She looked at me and smiled, then reached up a hand slowly to push back her long, straight hair. Of all the women I had seen, Tahereh's mother was the thinnest and tallest. She didn't say much, and I had never heard her laugh out loud. She walked as though she were gliding. Each time I saw her I thought of small waves in the sea that came softly, washing over the seashells and retreating slowly. To my twelve-year-old eyes, Tahereh's mother was the most beautiful woman I had ever seen.

As though she had suddenly become cold, she drew her *chador* up and said, "Are you here to see Tahereh? Come in. She is saying her prayers."

She leaned on the door. The gems on her pendant earrings were like pomegranate seeds.

There was an acrid smell inside. Tahereh was standing in the middle of the room. She was wearing a flowered *chador* that went to the floor. I could only see the round of her face, which was looking intently at the ceiling. There were no chairs in the room. I sat on the floor and leaned against the wall. Now Tahereh was looking at her feet.

I was so preoccupied with her prayers that I didn't notice her father at first. Thin and swarthy, knees drawn up to his chest, he was sitting in the other corner of the room smoking. I started to say hello, but then I saw that his eyes were closed.

Tahereh's mother remained in the doorway with her back to the room.

I tilted my head to see if the windows of our house were visible or not. They weren't. I busied myself watching Tahereh and thinking that if Grandmother knew that Tahereh recited her daily prayers, what would she say?

Tahereh was the only non-Armenian in our town who didn't make Grandmother's brows furrow. In the presence of Grandmother, no one was permitted to speak sloppy Armenian or to introduce a word of Persian. Tahereh spoke with Grandmother and the principal and the teachers as though she were reading from an Armenian textbook. She came with us to church on Sundays, and, just like Grandmother, closed her eyes firmly, knelt to pray, and crossed herself. She knew all the prayers and hymns by heart.

I could never concentrate in church. I played with the candle wax that dripped onto my hand, or stared at the light from the stained-glass windows illuminating the painting of Jesus and Mary that hung over the altar. The smell of incense made me sleepy and when I was startled out of my daze, my gaze immediately would be drawn to Tahereh, earnestly praying or listening intently to the priest. I used to feel ashamed and tell myself, *Edmond, you're not a real Christian!* The same thing that Grandmother said of everyone, either to their face or behind their backs. Then I'd take a deep breath and try to pull myself together to become a real Christian, but in that very moment, no matter where she was sitting in that little church, Tahereh would turn in my direction and wink or pull a face. I'd laugh aloud, forgetting the priest and church and faith completely. I was always being nudged by Mother or Grandmother for laughing inappropriately in church. And when I looked at Tahereh again, it was as though nothing had happened; she was staring at the altar, or her eyes were closed in prayer.

Grandmother often rebuked us. "Shame on you if you have to learn about religion and faith from the Muslim janitor's daughter." But one day, as we were leaving the church after the service, she noticed that Tahereh was wearing a little cross around her neck, and her eyes filled with tears. She kissed Tahereh on the forehead and after that day I never heard her say "the Muslim janitor's daughter" again.

Tahereh's mother was still looking out of the door. She was barefoot and the wind made waves of her long black skirt. Her bare calves were very pale. They looked ghost-like; if I put out my hand to touch them, it would surely go straight through them.

At parties, when the talk turned to the school janitor, my father and the other men used to say, "What a shame that a woman like that is chained to such a crazy dope addict." My mother and the other women would pretend not to hear.

On the day that Tahereh's father beat her mother and the commotion brought us running out to the school courtyard, my father wanted to intervene but Mother got angry. "What's it to you? If she wasn't so pretty would you still care?"

Tahereh's father was still dozing. I was thinking what an ugly man he was when suddenly Tahereh whipped off her *chador*, dashed across the room, said, "Race you!" and took off running.

By the time I was up and out of the room, Tahereh had already reached the grave of the priest and was skipping around the stone. Tahereh never just walked. She ran, or skipped, or jumped. No boy was as good at skipping as she was.

When I got to the grave, I said, "Your prayers didn't work."

Tahereh snickered. I wondered why she was laughing.

On the days that she came to do our laundry, Effat always said at sundown, "I have to go, or my prayers will be late."

Mother had once said, "Why don't you pray here?"

Effat answered, "No, ma'am, I mustn't."

One morning when I was playing cops and robbers by myself among the hanging sheets and towels on the ground floor, I asked Effat, "Why can't you pray here?"

Effat tightened the scarf around her head, looked around her once, and said in a low voice, "I just can't, dear! There is a cross in this house. My prayers will be invalidated!"

To Tahereh I said, "I meant that your prayers will be invalidated. You can't wear a cross when you're praying!"

She put a hand on her hip. "Who said I have a cross?"

"You do!" I insisted. "I've seen it myself."

She put a finger through the chain on her neck and held it out in front of her. "Come here and look."

A small Allah hung from the chain.

I asked, "Where's the cross?"

She swung her braid behind her head and laughed. "For school and church, I wear the cross. For prayers, it's Allah."

Together we scrambled up to sit on the priest's gravestone.

"Why do you have both a cross and an Allah?" I asked.

She shrugged and swung her legs. "Because they're both pretty." Then suddenly she said, "Hey, what about…"

I lowered my head. "It died."

She tilted her head. "Poor thing."

For a few moments she stopped swinging her legs. Then she put her hand in her pocket and pulled out a sweet bun, broke it in two, and held out half for me.

I didn't want to think about the ladybug anymore. I showed Tahereh the big toothless mouth. Now that I wasn't alone, I didn't feel afraid. Not of the gaping mouth, not of the church, not of the graveyard behind it.

Tahereh wolfed down the bun and started to laugh.

Sometimes I thought that Tahereh really was a sorcerer. Of all the people I knew, she was the only one I didn't need to explain things to. Like the baby frogs that were hidden in the grass by the harbor, or the one particular sunflower seed which didn't look like the rest. Other people couldn't see the angels and demons I saw in the clouds, and laughed at me. My mother didn't laugh, but I had to show her exactly where they were and even then they didn't seem to be of much interest to her. For Tahereh, everything was interesting. Shapes in the clouds, baby frogs, and even difficult words in Persian and Armenian. Sometimes she found stones on the beach that looked like people or animals, and which were more beautiful than the stones I found. The most important thing was that Tahereh wasn't afraid of anything. I had learned from storybooks that only sorcerers were fearless.

Tahereh pointed to the principal's window and said, "It's just like a loose tooth. It's hanging there just like his loose leg." And she giggled again. One slat of the shutter in the principal's window hung forward in the breeze.

I didn't laugh. Like all children at our school, I couldn't bring myself to laugh at the principal, even when he wasn't around. Tahereh was the only one who wasn't scared of him. She limped behind his back, making fun of the way he walked, and when she talked to him, she never flushed like the rest of us or started stuttering. The principal treated her differently than the rest of the students, too. He forced himself to reply to our greetings and never let us get away with even the smallest mistake, but he was always kind to Tahereh. We noticed that he smiled one of his rare smiles when he was talking to her, his face losing its perpetually stern, somber expression and almost seeming friendly. When he pushed the straight black hair away from his forehead with his long bony fingers, I thought of the fragility of the seashells that I had found on the shore.

When talk turned to the principal, my mother and the other ladies said, "What a shame that such a handsome man is crippled." My father and his friends used to grow quiet, and then someone would cough and change the subject.

Tahereh looked at my head. I waited for her to laugh but she didn't. "You did the right thing by shaving it. It will be much easier to wash your hair now."

She tossed her braids over her shoulder and took a deep breath. "I wish I could shave all my hair off

like you. I hate having my hair washed. It hurts."
One could never predict what Tahereh would say
or do next.

She jumped down from the gravestone and said,
"Come on, let's play hide and seek."

It was getting dark.

"Okay," I said. Then I hesitated. "But the graveyard is off limits."

Tahereh's eyes sparkled. "You hide wherever you
want and I'll hide wherever I want. Close your eyes!"

I put my head down on the gravestone, closed
my eyes, and counted to 100. When I opened my
eyes and stood up, it had grown darker, and the
light from the two windows seemed even brighter.
The wooden door of the janitor's room moved. I
thought maybe Tahereh had gone in there. As I got
closer, I heard voices.

Tahereh's mother said, "Are you imagining things
again? I've told you a hundred times, he hasn't laid
a hand on me."

The voice of Tahereh's father was garbled. "You
told me but I don't believe you. You're waiting for me
to die. Dream on! I have no intention of dying, and
he would never marry you anyway, not in a million
years. I know these people. They take up all the air
and then act as though we don't even exist."

I heard the sound of Tahereh's mother crying and then the door opened wide. I felt I had done something wrong and pressed myself to the wall. Tahereh's mother had taken off her *chador* and the light from the room shone on half her face. She looked like the picture of an angel I had won from the priest one Sunday. When she saw me she wiped away her tears with one hand, then with the same hand she stroked my face. "Are you looking for Tahereh? She must be around here somewhere."

A breeze blew across my face, drying the moisture from her tears. I took a few steps away from the wall, and then I turned and ran.

When I reached the first gravestone in the back courtyard, I stopped and looked around. There was no sign of Tahereh. The long grass swayed in the wind making the graves seem to appear and disappear.

I said to myself, "Don't be afraid! Tahereh is hiding behind one of these gravestones."

I called out, "Tahereh!"

There was no answer. I wanted to go back, but I froze. It was just like in my dreams when I wanted to run but couldn't.

I looked at the statue of the merchant's wife, sitting in the middle of the grass. Her head was bent over her book, which was obscured by the darkness.

I felt a hand on my shoulder and turned, thinking it must be Tahereh. It wasn't. It was someone much taller than us. I raised my head and saw a pair of stern eyes and a bony hand that pushed back the hair on its forehead.

A choking sound emerged from my mouth. It was like the whimper of a dog that's been muzzled. I turned to escape. The grass rustled and my eyes fell on the statue of the merchant's wife, who I saw had raised her head and was staring at me. Then she lifted her hand and pulled her stone shawl over her shoulder. I couldn't breathe.

I pushed past the principal and ran.

It was as if I was outside of my own body. My legs moved, a muffled whine escaped from my lips, my eyes saw the head of the merchant's wife and the somber face of the principal, and my hands clenched into fists that beat on the door of our house. As soon as my mother opened it, I passed out.

A bowl of water sat on the bedside table. My mother dipped in a handkerchief, which she wrung out and draped over my forehead.

My father was pacing in the room. "He didn't say what happened?"

My mother's gold bangles jingled. "No. He was just very afraid. He has a fever."

"I don't understand why he's afraid of everything!"

"Are you starting this again? He's a child, for heaven's sake."

"A twelve-year-old boy is a child? When I was twelve, I was a terror!"

My mother's bangles clanged against the bowl of water. "And you're still a terror! Thank God Edmond doesn't take after you in character or in looks."

My father was a short, heavy man who did not like to be reminded that he was short and heavy. He sat on my chair and put his feet on my desk. My mother hated it when people put their feet upon tables. My father kicked the desk hard several times. "I know it was that Muslim janitor's girl who scared him. For Christ's sake! A twelve-year-old boy shouldn't be scared by a little girl. When I was twelve…this is all your fault! Haven't I said he shouldn't play with her? It's a good thing you only have this sissy boy to look after. He's always either in the street or in other people's houses."

The damp handkerchief itched my forehead. My mother said, "Jesus Christ, he's started again."

My father was still wounded by my mother's words about his appearance. "Why can't you learn from Shakeh? She's bringing up four kids, but they're always clean and polite, and so is her house. Arsham is two years younger than Edmond and he goes hunting with his father. You only have one kid, and he dies of fear if he sees a rabbit."

Mother's bangles stopped jangling. Nothing he could have said could have hurt her more. My mother had never managed to get pregnant again after me and even her own sister would say to her from time to time, "Stop smoking cigarettes and trying to read your future in the coffee grounds at the bottom of your cup, and look after your house for a change."

My father was still talking. "I'm sure it was the janitor's daughter. Don't let me hear about him playing with her again."

My mother pressed the handkerchief so hard on my forehead that it hurt. I thought that if they knew it wasn't Tahereh's fault, they would still let me see her after school. I tried to think of an excuse to exonerate Tahereh without also mentioning my run-in with the principal.

I cried out, "The graves…"

My mother jumped. "Holy Mary, Mother of God!"

My father sat silently for a few moments. Then under his breath he grumbled, "A thousand times

I've said that this broken-down area is no place to live. He has a graveyard instead of a playground."

My mother stroked my face. She pulled the covers up to my chin and said, "Sleep now, my darling. Sleep."

She stood, picked up the bowl of water, and went towards the door of my room. As she passed in front of my father, she said, "And *I* have said a thousand times, whenever you buy another house, I'll rent this place out and we can move."

Through my half-closed eyes, I saw that my father was chewing on his moustache and following my mother with his eyes as she left the room.

I hid my head under the covers. When I emerged again, the lamp had been switched off and the door was closed. I was tired but couldn't sleep. Where had Tahereh hidden? Had I been scared of the graves or of the principal? Why had it seemed that the statue of the merchant's wife had lifted its head? I thought of my mother's sister's claims that Father wanted to claw Mother away from her house. But the merchant's wife *had* been looking at me. She looked like someone. I remembered the tear-drenched face of Tahereh's mother and the words of her father. "I know these people." Which people did he mean? Why had Tahereh's mother cried? Why wasn't I like Arsham who loved to go hunting? Why couldn't people see the shapes in the clouds? Surely I had only imagined the hand of the merchant's wife adjusting her shawl? The rhythmic jingling of my mother's bangles coming from the sitting room lulled me to sleep.

The next day my mother wouldn't let me go to school and brought me breakfast in bed. She had made soft-boiled eggs with buttered toast and hot cocoa; all my favorite things, which my mother seldom had the patience to make for me. She sat facing me on the edge of the bed.

After each spoonful of egg or gulp of cocoa, I said, "Thank you."

It was as though by thanking her again and again I was apologizing. Each time my parents fought because of me, I felt guilty. My mother stroked my face a few times and straightened out the bedcovers.

Finally she said, "Enough! Why do you keep thanking me?" She turned her head towards the window.

I knew that from where she was sitting, she could see the mossy tiles of the church roof and a piece of the sky, which was cloudy that day. Suddenly my heart caught and I began to cry. My mother held me tightly for a few moments. Then she got up, picked up the breakfast tray and left the room. Her eyes were red.

As usual, I felt numb when I had finished crying. I pulled the covers up to my chin and looked out of the window. From where I was lying, I could see the principal's window with its closed shutters. I wondered if it was possible that he had forgotten about what had happened yesterday. My oldest cousin was now in his last year of high school and often told us stories about his time at the elementary school and the principal's punishments. If my grandmother overheard, she would say, "That's exactly right. Children must be disciplined properly."

The principal had moved to our town a few months before my parents' marriage, and most of the Armenians saw him for the first time at my parents' wedding.

One time I overheard my mother say to her sister, "When I walked into the hall in my wedding gown, he was sitting there, facing the door and smoking a cigarette. He looked just like a painting, like he'd come from another planet, far away, or from a time past."

My aunt laughed. "So that's why you turned around and went to the bathroom and cried for half an hour?"

"Don't be ridiculous," my mother said, and tried to laugh, but it sounded forced.

The principal had no family or close friends in our community. He rarely accepted social invitations and spent most of his time after school in his room. Other than Tahereh's mother, who cleaned his room, the priest was one of the very few people who ever visited him and spent any amount of time there. My grandmother said that before moving here, the principal had wanted to be a priest himself. I had often seen him coming and going to the church at night.

My mother, smiling gently, used to sigh, "Such a godly man."

My father snickered. "What a foolish man! There are better things to do at night." And he'd pinch my mother's cheek and laugh. My mother reacted as though there were a roach on my father's hand and shoved it away. This only made my father laugh louder.

The sound of the school bell woke me with a start. I got up and stood by the window. The children were playing in the schoolyard. Anush, hand on her hip, was arguing with one of the boys. Tahereh was there too but she didn't look up at my window once. The bell rang again and the children formed lines for each class. The principal stood at the front and spoke to them. Tahereh's mother went up and down the steps a few times carrying trays of tea. School ended and the children went home. Then the teachers left, too, and Tahereh's mother went back up the stairs with a broom and dustpan. Defeated, I sat on my bed and thought that I didn't have a single friend, when Mother suddenly popped her head into the room. "Tahereh is here to see you."

I jumped joyfully off the bed.

Mother rocked back and forth on her feet. "Don't tell your father."

I squirmed inwardly with joy and tried to figure out what I wanted to show Tahereh first: my books, or my toys?

Tahereh came in. She glanced around the room and went straight over to the window. She was wearing her navy-blue school uniform. The back of the skirt was faded to a different color than the rest of the uniform.

I searched for something to say. "The back of your skirt is dirty," I offered.

She drew a large X with her finger on the window. "It's not dirty. It's just worn out."

Then she came over and sat on the edge of the bed. "We spread out our bedding every night and roll it up again in the morning."

She picked up the book on my nightstand and started to flip through it.

"Take it!" I said. "It's yours. I have two copies."

She put the book down and stood up. "I have to go," she said, and left.

The next day I waited for the principal's summons but nothing happened. When I saw him in the hallway and said a timid hello, he just nodded without looking at me and walked past. His thoughts were clearly elsewhere. I said to myself that if this mood lasted a few more days, I was in the clear.

The days passed, and the Easter holiday began.

My aunt and uncle on my mother's side were coming from Abadan to stay with us. As usual, they came with their arms full of gifts. For me there were little colored stickers to paste on the Easter eggs, for Father there was an English hunting knife, and for mother there was a beaded evening bag and a big box of fresh sour cherries. That night all of the family came over. My mother was overjoyed to see her sister and kept laughing happily. After dinner she put a huge bowl of the cherries on the table and said, "Poor me, what am I to do with all these sour cherries?"

My uncle pointed to us children, who were attacking them hungrily. "With this cloud of locusts, they'll be gone in two days."

Mother yelled, "That's enough! You're going to get stomach aches."

Grandmother pushed aside the burnt cutlet on her plate with the tip of her fork and said, "What big cherries. They'd make a nice jam."

My mother was in such a good mood that she agreed with Grandmother. "What a good idea! I'll make jam with the rest of them."

I saw my grandmother and Auntie look at each other and smirk. Mother's lips formed into a thin line, and from the way she jumped from her seat, picked up the bowl of cherries, and repeated, "I'm going to make them into jam," I knew she had seen, too.

The next day Mother asked me, "Will you help me pit the cherries?"

Her sister had gone off to visit Auntie Shakeh. My mother had complained of a headache as an excuse not to go.

"Yes," I said, "as long as I can play with the pits."

"As long as you don't make a mess," my mother answered.

I sunk a crochet needle into a cherry. The stone popped out and fell into the bowl under my hands. Red juice spilled over my fingers. I was a brave commander who killed the enemy soldiers with a single mighty blow from a spear and tossed aside their bodies one by one.

In a book that my father read from time to time, and whose photos my mother had forbidden me to look at, there was a strange picture. It was a photo of a hill made out of people's skulls. I wasn't even old enough to go to school the first time I saw it.

I asked my father, "What is this picture of?"

"The heads of the Armenians who were murdered by the Ottomans," he replied.

Mother had arrived at exactly that moment and yelled at my father, "Stop! He's a child, you'll frighten him."

Father, still staring at the photo, said, "Child or adult, everyone has to know what tragedy befell his people."

When I got older I understood why each year we celebrated my birthday, which was 24 April,* a few days early or a few days late. Grandmother and Mrs. Grigorian fasted each year on 24 April, went to church, and lit candles.

The scent of the warm jam wafted through the

house as I made a little hill with the sour cherry stones.

In the afternoon Mother put a jar of jam in my hands and said, "Take this to the principal."

I hadn't heard anything from Tahereh for a few days. New toys and the holiday ritual of visiting and receiving visitors had filled my days. I missed her. I jumped up to go.

My mother pointed to the corner of the room. "First clean up those pits."

Jam in hand, I went through the open school gates. There was no one in the courtyard. When I got close to the janitor's room, I peeped in. Tahereh's father was sitting in a corner of the room. His head was leaning against the wall and his eyes were closed. An acrid smell was seeping from the room. Tahereh wasn't there. Neither was her mother. I turned my head up to the window of the principal's room and paused. Suddenly I remembered why I had come. In the excitement of possibly seeing Tahereh, I had forgotten to be afraid of seeing the principal again. I thought to myself, *There's nothing to be afraid of. I'm a big boy. I got good marks in my exams, and I'm almost done with my Easter homework.*

I climbed the wooden stairs. The hallway of the upper floor was half dark. How different it was from those times when there were children shouting and running through it. It was as if I was seeing this hallway for the first time. On one side a long rail faced the courtyard with some plaster columns covered in students' graffiti. On the other side were the doors to the classrooms. The wooden floor creaked beneath my feet. Why had I never heard this sound before? The closer I got to the principal's room, the more my old fear of him returned.

I said to myself, *I hope he's not there. But what if he is? I will say hello, then I will say, "My mother sent this jam for you." I will put the jar in his hand, say goodbye, and leave. What if he doesn't put his hand out? Then I will put the jar on the table. Which table?* It was as though I was writing a composition for the principal rather than planning to speak to him.

I realized that I had never seen the principal's room before. Tahereh had seen it. She said he had a lot of books. The walls were covered from floor to ceiling with filled bookshelves. She told me there was also a big cross on the wall. I asked Tahereh if the principal had read all those books. Tahereh said, "I'm sure he has." She said that the principal always sat in his room either reading a book or writing.

Sometimes he got down on his knees in front of the cross and prayed.

As I got closer to the room I saw that the door was half open. I knew that I should knock on the door but the sound of crying that came from within startled me, and I forgot that eavesdropping was a nasty thing to do. I peeked round the door into the room. The first thing I saw was the big cross on the wall, and then the books. They were in the bookcases that filled the room, on the floor, on the large table in the middle of the room. The principal sat behind the table with his head in his hands.

A woman was sitting at the table, too. In the twilight I could only see her profile. She reminded me of the painting of the Holy Mary hanging above the altar in the church. She played with a corner of her *chador*, talking while she cried. I couldn't hear what she said. Her voice was calm and weary, like when she spoke to me and Tahereh. I knew I mustn't stand there, but I stayed anyway.

The principal got up. He put his hands in his pockets. Then he took them out. With one hand he pushed the hair off his forehead. With the other he closed the book that was on the table. Then he walked towards Tahereh's mother.

I heard a noise behind me. The wooden floor of the hallway creaked beneath someone's footsteps.

I turned around.

It was Tahereh's father. I hid myself behind one of the pillars.

Tahereh's father walked heavily towards the principal's room. There was something long and shiny in his hands and he used this to push open the door.

For a few moments I heard only the sound of the wind in the hallway. Then suddenly there was an eruption of sound. Weeping and shouting and things crashing to the floor.

I froze behind the pillar. I felt that something very bad was about to happen. I imagined I was going home. In my mind I crossed the school courtyard, then our own courtyard; the stairs, the balcony. Now I was in my room. It was like those nights when I woke up thirsty and still half asleep, thought I had gotten out of bed and gone to the kitchen for a drink of water, but in reality I was still in bed.

Suddenly I felt thirsty.

I heard the sound of breaking glass and of something being thrown into the school courtyard. Tahereh's mother screamed, the principal said something in a low voice and Tahereh's father yelled, "I'm going to kill you both!"

I backed further away, sat on the floor, and stared at the plaster pillar. There was something written at the bottom of it that had been scratched out, then there was a plus sign, then another name after it had been scratched out, followed by an equal symbol and a heart with an arrow through it. I heard footsteps tap-tap on the stairs. Several people ran by me: my parents, and my aunt and uncle. I closed my eyes.

My father and uncle were shouting, "Stop it, you crazy bastard!"

I heard my mother shout. "This is all that woman's fault!" Then I heard the sound of a slap, Tahereh's mother crying, my parents talking and the sound of my aunt muttering under her breath, "Oh my God."

I focused on the pierced heart at the bottom of the pillar. I wondered whose initials they were? Who loved whom? Who didn't want anyone to know who loved whom? The door of the principal's room burst open and my father and uncle dragged Tahereh's father out, who was crying. Behind them came my aunt, pushing Tahereh's mother in front of her.

I poked my head out from behind the pillar and watched them until they had gone down the stairs. At the end of the hallway I noticed a shadow. It was Tahereh. I got up to go over to her but she vanished.

A wind blew through the hall.

I looked into the principal's room. He was sitting on his chair with his eyes closed. My mother stood next to him.

Everything was quiet.

My mother wiped the principal's forehead with a white handkerchief and said, "You should not concern yourself. It is not your doing." My mother never spoke such articulate Armenian, not even in front of my grandmother.

The principal didn't move. Then he opened his eyes and stared at the cross on the wall.

My mother hesitated for a few moments. Then she crumpled up the handkerchief and walked towards the door.

I backed away. My foot caught on something. I looked. It was the broken jar of jam. Red syrup was spilling onto the wooden floor of the hallway.

When I looked up I was face to face with my mother. She started. Then she quickly smoothed her hair with her hand. She opened her mouth as if to say something but I backed away and ran.

Tahereh wasn't in the courtyard. I looked through the window of their room. Her father sat curled up in one corner. Her mother sat in another corner, crying.

I moved away from the window. I felt terrible

and wanted to cry. I put my head down and walked away. With the tip of my foot I kicked around the sand. When I looked up again I saw that I was in the graveyard behind the church. Tahereh was sitting on the grass next to one of the graves. I went over to her and sat down. She was tearing a long stalk of grass into tiny bits.

Without looking at me she asked, "Aren't you scared?"

She plucked a few more blades of grass. "I never understand why you're scared of this place," she went on. "These people are dead. There's nothing to be afraid of from the dead. They can't beat you. They can't bother you. But my father beats my mother and me. He won't leave us alone. I'm afraid of my father. No – I'm not afraid of him, I hate him. I wish he were dead!" She raised her hand to her cheek. I looked at her. She was crying.

I had never seen her cry before. I put my hand on her shoulder. She jerked away, got up, and left. There was something odd about the way she was walking. I sat there for a while, tearing up stalks of grass.

When I got home, my mother didn't look at me; she just told me to wash my hands, eat my dinner, and go to bed. From my bed, I heard voices in the sitting room.

My aunt said, "Unbelievable! I can't believe you would take the side of such a woman."

"I'm not taking her side," my father said. "I just know she isn't that type of woman."

My aunt laughed. "You know? How?"

My uncle said, "So it was this principal of yours who—"

I heard my mother's bangles jangling. "Does anyone want tea?"

"Oh my God!" my aunt exclaimed. "I've never heard of such things."

Just as I was about to fall asleep, I suddenly realized why Tahereh's way of walking looked so odd to me. It was the first time I had seen her walk slowly and without any hurry. She wasn't running or jumping or skipping, and I, for the first time, hadn't been scared to be alone in the graveyard behind the church.

PART II

seashells

IT WAS THE DAY BEFORE EASTER.

At lunch, Alenush said, "Behzad and I have decided to get married." Just as if she were saying, "Could you please pass the salt?"

Martha froze for a few moments. Then she began to roll small pieces of soft bread into tiny balls.

We'd been sitting like this at the table when the news of Grandmother's death had reached us. That day, too, when I had hung up the receiver and said, "It was Arsham. Grandmother…" Martha had not moved for a few moments. Then she had started to pile up the balls of bread into a little heap on the side of her plate. We had known for a long time that Grandmother was dying. And we had been waiting for some time to hear this news from our daughter.

Alenush turned to face me. "Dad, can you please pass the salt?"

Martha continued to ball up her bread. I looked at my untouched food and carefully put my spoon back down on my plate. A loud cry drifted in from the lane: "Scrap iron, water heaters!" The things peddlers wanted to buy had changed so much since the old days.

When we had first come to Tehran, each time we heard the cry, "Coats, pants, jackets!" Mother would say to me, "Edmond, go call him."

Grandmother, if she heard about this (and she always heard about it) would frown. "But that wasn't even old! It could still be worn." Or she would shake her head ruefully and say, "That beautiful china! Those copper bowls, mementoes of our dearly departed."

"Our dearly departed" was my father's father, but my mother was the enemy both of old things and of all keepsakes that came from my father's family. My mother would shrug at Grandmother's disapproving outbursts and her lips would form a single thin line.

My grandmother and aunt, when they thought I was busy playing, would gossip behind my mother's back. "Our Lady of Perpetual Whims. Nothing has any value to her."

The peddler cried, "Doors and aluminum windows, gas canisters, refrigerators, TVs! We buy it all!"

Alenush pushed back her chair. "I've got to go. I'm already late for class."

She looked at Martha. Then at me. Then back at Martha. Then at me. I tried to smile. Alenush chewed her lip and tilted her head. Just like when she was a child and was trying to say, without words, that she was sorry for whatever kind of mischief she'd made. I wished this were just another one of her childish pranks. But I knew it wasn't. When the door closed, there was a little heap of bread balls on Martha's plate.

I got up from the table and walked over to stand by the glass doors facing the garden. The violets in the flower bed this year were all yellow. I asked, "What color were the violets last year?"

Martha said, "Edmond, I beg of you, talk to her. Please!"

She hadn't cried this bitterly even when Grandmother died.

I sat down in an armchair and looked out at the violets. *Behzad and I have decided to get married.* I pictured their faces: my cousin Arsham, my other cousins, their husbands and wives, the whole family... My aunt! I tried to guess what their reaction would be: first disbelief, then shock, then silence, then...

Years before, when the daughter of one of our relatives had married an Englishman, Grandmother and Auntie Shakeh had refused to visit them until the birth of their daughter.

A strong wind gusted through the garden and all of the violets bent over in the direction in which it blew. I thought what a relief it was that Grandmother was no longer with us. Who would have had the heart to tell her that the light of her life wanted to marry a non-Armenian? Possibly only Alenush herself.

One night, when Alenush was about seven or eight, she had come down in her white nightdress, hair loose around her shoulders, to say goodnight before going to bed. Grandmother was staying with us.

Martha said, "Don't forget to brush your teeth and say your evening prayers."

Alenush, her back to us and facing the door, shrugged and said, "I don't feel like it."

Grandmother retorted, "If you don't brush your teeth, they'll fall out."

Alenush turned and stared at her. "I didn't mean brushing my teeth," she said. "I meant I don't feel like praying."

Grandmother sat up straight in her chair. "Praying is our way of giving thanks to God. For all of the blessings He has bestowed on us; for creating us."

Alenush opened the door. "I didn't ask Him to create me, so why should I thank Him?"

Martha scolded her. "Alenush!"

Grandmother said slowly, "Leave it, she's only a child."

After that, each Sunday in church, Grandmother seated Alenush next to herself and when the services were over she gave her pictures of saints or a colorful rosary or a small gold or silver cross. A few years later, at Christmas, Alenush painted a large picture of Jesus for Grandmother, and all around the edge were pasted the pictures and rosaries Grandmother had given her.

When I asked why she hadn't put the crosses on the painting, she replied, "I'm keeping those; they're so shiny and pretty."

The violets were still being bent this way and that by the wind. The wall clock in the hallway chimed three times. I remembered my meeting with Danique. *She must be waiting for me*, I thought. Signing two hundred second-term report cards was the last thing I felt like doing right now. *What do I feel like doing right now?* I wondered. *Just sit here and look at the violets.* I dialed the school's number.

With the second ring, I heard Danique's voice in the receiver. "Adab Armenian School. May I help you?"

"Mrs. Vice-Principal, don't you know what it means to be on vacation?" I teased.

She laughed. "Don't you know how to be punctual, Mr. Principal?" she joked back.

"Can you sign the report cards on my behalf?"

Her voice became serious. "Are you not feeling well, Edmond?"

"I'm fine, but…"

I could just imagine what she was doing: removing her clip-on earring, gluing the phone to her ear, and, with the pen that was unfailingly in her hand, starting to draw elaborate doodles on the piece of paper that was always on her desk. "Is Martha all right, then? Alenush?"

I took a deep breath. "We're all fine. I'll tell you about it another time."

I heard her let out a sigh of relief. "Don't worry about the report cards. It's just…they called from the North. The textbooks are ready. But there's no one who can bring them to Tehran. Should we wait until after the holiday?"

I couldn't think. We'd been waiting for those books for several months now, but…I just couldn't think. "I'll call you back, Danique. And…thanks."

I imagined her face, the thin eyebrows raised, giving her pale, round face an expression of surprise, but all she said was, "*Thanks?* For what?" I hung up.

I returned to the sitting room, sat down again facing the garden and the violets, and wondered what I would do without Danique. I remembered our first meeting. She had come to my office for an interview. Alenush wasn't even one yet. In those days Danique was still thin and her hair still black, and she wore it down around her shoulders.

I asked, "Do you have any experience working in a school?"

Just then Adamian dragged two boys into the office by their ears, both of them sweating and crying. I didn't have much patience for Adamian: he was the school supervisor and loved to give lengthy reports on each and every banal occurrence in the schoolyard. I cut him off before he could begin. "What was the fight about?"

Adamian let go of the boys' ears, coughed his sententious cough, clasped his hands behind his back, rocked back and forth on his feet a few times and finally said, "Over a dime that they found in the lane. Please take into consideration, sir…"

One of the boys, still in tears, interrupted him. "I swear to God, I found it first, sir!"

The second one cried, "Liar! I found it first."

"Silence!" shouted Adamian.

I was trying to figure out how to resolve this expediently when Danique reached into her purse. Her hair fell over her bag and I couldn't see what she was doing. My attention was caught by an ornament hanging from the handle of her purse. Before I could figure out if it was a cat or a bear, Adamian started again. "I've said many times that the children who lie come from families who…"

This time it was Danique who interrupted Adamian. She snapped her purse shut and asked me, "May I?"

Not waiting for my answer, she looked at the children and asked, "Where's the dime?"

She took the offered coin and put a nickel in each of the children's hands. "Half and half. Okay?"

The astonished look on Adamian's face was priceless. The boys looked at each other. Adamian coughed a few times but before he could say anything, I said, "The matter is resolved, Mr. Adamian." I looked at my watch. "Isn't it time to ring the bell for class?"

Adamian looked indignantly at Danique and put a hand on each of the boys' shoulders. "Off with you!"

Danique said, "Wait a minute, please."

The metal donation box on my desk was labeled "Help the Needy Children." Danique held it out to the boys.

As soon as the door closed, I started to laugh. "Can you start tomorrow then?"

Her laugh echoed in the office. "Why not right now?"

In all these years, how often had I said to Martha, "What would I do without Danique?"

Martha laughed. "She's just wonderful. Wonderful!"

From the first time they met, Martha and Danique had become close friends. I was surprised. There was almost nothing they agreed on. Whenever they discussed an issue, like the responsibilities of women and commitments of men, they would argue, and Alenush, who always took Danique's side, would laugh herself sick. Danique and Martha had completely different tastes in clothes as well. Alenush always criticized the dark clothes her mother wore and would say, "Auntie Danique wears lovely bright colors." Martha would frown and say, "Women ought to wear clothes that suit their age." But then, as if she had suddenly developed a guilty conscience, she'd laugh. "Bright colors really do suit Danique, but not me."

I had asked Martha a few times, "Have you never asked Danique why she left Tabriz for Tehran?"

Martha shrugged. "If she had wanted to tell me, she would have by now."

"But haven't you at least asked why she never married?"

Martha laughed. "You of all people shouldn't

press the point. If she gets married and her husband doesn't want her to work, what will you do?"

I knew she was dodging the question. Wanting to know the reason for Danique not marrying was not just to satisfy my curiosity. I wanted to have a convincing answer to give the constant stream of suitors who approached me with bids of courtship for Danique from among our friends, acquaintances, family members, and even the teachers at school. The day that I learned the reason for Danique not marrying, Martha said, "Please don't say anything. Please let her tell you herself." But Danique never said a word.

Like every year, we were invited to my aunt Shakeh's house for Easter dinner. Martha didn't come out of the bedroom until it was time to go. Alenush got back from the university just in time to change her jeans for a slightly newer pair and to brush her long, straight hair. Martha came downstairs. She did not tell Alenush to *Please put on a skirt.* I leaned against the coat rack in the hallway. Alenush looked at her mother and chewed on her lip.

Martha started towards the door. "Hurry up. Auntie Shakeh will be getting worried." On the white collar of her dress she had fastened a small ruby brooch.

Martha and I were sitting in the garden of Café Naderi* when I put the ruby brooch on the table and said, "Will you marry me?"

Martha ran a finger over the ruby a few times. Then she raised her head and laughed. "What a bright red stone!"

Her gaze was set on something in the garden. An Italian singer with a thick accent was singing one of Vigen's* famous songs. "Oh moonlight, lovers' companion…" My heart was in my throat.

When she looked back at me she said, "Have you ever wondered where they get such red watermelons from?" She nodded towards the waiters who were carrying large platters of watermelon slices. Among the greenness of the trees in the garden, the deep red of the fruit looked even redder.

The orchestra had gathered up its instruments, the fountain in the middle of the pool had been turned off, the waiters were folding up the white tablecloths, and I was still talking. "My grandmother is very particular. About cleanliness and housekeeping, and customs and traditions. More than anything, she cares about speaking proper Armenian and about religious beliefs. My mother, on the other hand, couldn't care less about most of that stuff and is easygoing about everything."

Martha lined up the watermelon seeds on her plate with the tip of her fork. "What an interesting woman."

"My mother?" I asked.

"No," she said. "Your grandmother."

When Alenush was born, Grandmother made Martha a gift of her own diamond engagement ring.

In our family, no one really understood the relationship between Grandmother and Martha. For the rest of the family, visiting Grandmother was an obligation; one undertaken out of respect or perhaps fear. But for Martha, visiting Grandmother was a favorite pastime. They would sit together for hours talking about knitting or cooking, or about Grandmother's youth or the proper way to perform religious ceremonies.

One day after Grandmother had visited, and had praised Martha's baking, Martha was washing up the baking tray when she said over her shoulder to me, "I wish I was your grandmother's daughter."

Alenush was eight or nine at the time. She glanced up from reading *Children's World* magazine and looked at me. "Would that mean you'd be married to your aunt?"

Martha stared at the water splashing over the tray for a few moments. Then she turned off the tap and said, "Nunush, it's past your bedtime."

Alenush, grumbling, left the kitchen. Martha leaned against the sink and began to dry the tray. "My mother, may she rest in peace, had no patience for the simple pleasures in life, like baking or sewing. Maybe that's why she was always restless." She put the tray away in the cupboard. "But the real joy in life lies in exactly those things – the little things – doesn't it?"

I leafed through *Children's World*, which Alenush had left on the table, gazing longest at the back page where Alenush's favorite series, *The Fearless Pilot*,* was printed.

In the car I put on some music that Martha liked. After a few minutes, she said, "Edmond, please turn that off." No one said anything until we got to my aunt's.

My aunt's house was as it always was on Easter nights. Arsham showed me the dyed eggs. "Remember how we used to fight over these?"

I was just thinking *Is there anything we didn't fight about?* when Arsham said, "Is there anything we didn't fight about?" and his plump body shook with laughter.

Arsham is two years younger than me. When we were kids, he was skinny and much taller than I was. All of the children, both in our family and at school, were in awe of him. He loved hunting and sports and any game that offered the possibility of breaking something. If we were left alone, he would yawn and make fun of my toys and collections. Almost every time we were together we fought. I don't know how old I was when we finally became friends. Maybe it was the day we went to the movies together. When the hero's best friend was killed we both cried, and when we got back home, we dueled with Grandmother's knitting needles, just like the hero and his buddy. For years now we had not just been cousins but also very good friends. For a moment I considered telling Arsham about Alenush.

I had just opened my mouth when Arsham picked up two colored eggs from the basket. He gave one to me and said, "What's the wager?"

I lifted up my egg and brought it down on the pointed round top of his egg. Nothing. His turn, and my egg broke under his blow.

Arsham laughed. "You still can't beat me."

Arsham's little daughter, chubby and curly-haired, arrived on the scene and said, "Playing with eggs is for kids, not for grown-ups."

She took the egg carefully from her father, put it back in the basket, and looked at me. "Uncle Edmond, now that your egg is broken, you don't need it anymore, do you?"

She took my egg, looked around furtively, put one finger to her lips and said, "Shhh…now I have five." Then she skipped out of the room.

Arsham started laughing. "Naughty child!"

"Like father, like daughter," I said.

He laughed harder. "You remember?"

One Easter, when we were children, we invented a game where whoever collected the most broken eggs was the winner. One year, Arsham had vanquished more eggs than usual but his own remained undamaged. Later he showed me the egg he'd used in the game. He had persuaded the neighborhood carpenter to make him a wooden egg, and Arsham had very cleverly painted it so that no one would know he was cheating.

The basket of colored eggs sat on a sideboard in the dining room. Next to it there was a big *paska** loaf topped with a chocolate cross, and *nazouk** pastries that my aunt had baked herself, and whenever someone praised them, she would say, "No, no, they don't hold a candle to Mother's." And there was sweet and salty *gata*,* and fruit and *iris** candy. There were two tall silver candlesticks that were placed on the sideboard and their white candles lit every Easter night and Epiphany. On the wall there was a large picture of Grandmother in a wooden frame with a black ribbon fastened diagonally across the photo.

While Grandmother was still alive, the whole family gathered at her house every Easter and Epiphany, even for those last two years when she was almost continually in bed, and the preparation of the rice and *kuku** and the smoked fish, as well as tending to the guests, was left to Auntie Shakeh. That final year, Grandmother had only been able to come to the table in her wheelchair for a few moments, just long enough to say the prayer before the meal and to take the holy wafer with us. For as long as I could remember, I had taken the holy wafer while Grandmother said a prayer, and my eyes would be fixed on her bony face with its high cheekbones, and her hair gathered in a bun at the back of her head. When I was a child I thought that if Grandmother wore a hooded cloak, she would look like the monks whose pictures we won as prizes from the priest in church on Sundays.

As always, Auntie Shakeh finished the prayer before dinner by remembering Grandmother. "May your pure spirit always be with us and protect us."

Martha, who was sitting next to Auntie, started to cry. Alenush stared at the flowered china plate and gripped the silver handle of her fork.

Auntie leaned over and said slowly to me, "Sometimes I think Martha loved Mother even more than I did."

One of the children ran into the room crying. "All of my eggs are broken!"

Arsham picked up the serving spoon for the rice. "God have mercy on those who have passed, and have a thought for the living, too."

Our cousin, who, according to Arsham, would laugh at the drop of a hat, started giggling. Auntie glared at her and the twenty people sitting around the table tried not to laugh, too. I looked at Martha and Alenush. It was as if neither of them were in the room.

My uncle's wife was saying, "They met at a friend's birthday party. A very respectable family. His father works for the NIOC.* They moved to Tehran only recently." She looked at her granddaughter. "You said he is studying what?"

Her granddaughter was a thin, shy girl who didn't say much; she was almost the same age as Alenush.

When they were children, Alenush had nicknamed her "Holy Mary."

Auntie said, "Congratulations, my dear." She looked at the photograph of Grandmother. "She was always so worried that the children would choose someone unsuitable. These days…"

The sound of glass breaking made everyone jump.

Martha pushed back her chair and bent over. "I'm sorry, it was my fault. My hand slipped. Be careful of the splinters, children."

Alenush didn't even raise her head.

Throughout dinner, Martha didn't say much, and Alenush made a little pile of rice and *kuku* on her plate.

When we were getting up from the table, Alenush squeezed my hand. "Dad, you have to talk to her. Please!"

We were visiting my childhood home in the North when we heard Behzad's name mentioned for the first time. Behzad, who was the smartest student in the faculty; Behzad, who had read so much; Behzad this, Behzad that. Martha just listened silently. It was April, and the perfume of the orange blossom was overwhelming.

Since our family left for Tehran, I had only returned to our coastal town a few times. Before my mother's death, we didn't visit because she had no desire to go back, then my father died, and then…I don't know why.

There wasn't much left on the upper or lower floors of the house, just some old furniture and chests full of odds and ends. Alenush rushed excitedly through the rooms. Only in my mother's room did she calm down for a few moments and look around.

She ran a hand over the broken foot of a mirrored wardrobe. "What a shame. Such a beautiful wardrobe."

It was part of my mother's mother's trousseau, and for years it had sat in one of the uninhabited rooms on the ground floor. Mother had no purpose for it, but she couldn't bear to throw it away either, until finally, one day, she found a use for it.

One afternoon, following an evening of fighting between my parents, the wardrobe came upstairs. I was used to my parents' bickering and arguing; usually it stopped at the point of saying hurtful things or, at most, yelling (though not very loudly) behind the closed door of their bedroom. But this night things had gotten out of hand. Behind the bedroom door, I heard the sound of things being thrown and breaking. Mother brought a pillow, blanket and mattress to my room and spent the night there. The next day when I got home from school, the door to the closet next to my room was open. In a corner, there was a single bed and facing it, the mirrored wardrobe. The closet, which had a window facing the courtyard of the school and church, was really a bedroom that we had never used before, but from that day on, it was known as "Mother's room."

My mother said to her sister, "A room of my own! Do you understand? It's all mine. It's the only place where I feel at peace."

Once Grandmother finally got used to this new arrangement, she would say to my aunt at least once every few days, "If only she spent half the time she does cleaning and tidying that room on the rest of the house…"

My mother, who hated sewing, made flowered curtains for her room and a matching bedspread out of the same fabric. On the shelf above her bed she arranged books and a few little boxes, each containing something: some locks of my baby hair; two of my milk teeth; her grandmother's silver thimble; a pair of socks from her own childhood. If she was in a good mood, she would let me come into her room. Behind the little table next to the window I would sit and do my homework. Mother's room always had a lovely smell and sitting behind that small table, I was ready to do a thousand pages of homework. Mother sat on a chair facing the window. She read a book or, with one hand under her chin, elbow on the windowsill, she looked out at the courtyard of the school and the graveyard beyond. Sometimes she sang under her breath. Sometimes she embroidered. She never showed her embroidery to anyone, but arranged a few pieces here and there in her own room, on the table or the arm of a chair or on the shelf above the bed. Maybe I was the only one who knew that she kept the rest of her embroidery ironed and carefully folded in a wooden chest in her room. The chest had a huge key that made a muffled ring when she turned it in the lock. Sometimes Mother allowed me to lock and unlock the chest so that I could hear that sound. On one of Martha's birthdays, Mother made a gift of the chest and all its embroidery to her.

Martha's face shone. "You made all of these?" Mother nodded. Grandmother and Auntie Shakeh's mouths dropped open in surprise.

Alenush looked into the wardrobe. "Behzad would love this. Here, take these!"

She thrust a few rusted hairpins into my hand and bent over again to reach for the broken leg of the wardrobe. "I wish Behzad were here, he'd know how to fix this."

I looked over at Martha, who stared at Alenush for a couple of seconds, then turned on her heel and left the room. The rust of the hairpins had rubbed off onto my palm.

My mother usually wore her hair loose over her shoulders. But on Sundays she would gather up her hair on top of her head with dozens of these pins. Each week, before church was even finished, the pins would begin to slip out of her hair and fall to her shoulders. One Sunday afternoon my grand-mother came for lunch at our house and pulled a pin out of her bowl of borscht. After that, Mother cut her hair short, once and for all.

Alenush emptied out the chests. "This is mine. This is for Behzad. Whoa, look at this fabric! I'm going to frame it."

Martha passed silently through the dimly lit rooms.

That afternoon, in the graveyard behind the church, I said to Alenush, "When can your mother and I meet Behzad?"

Martha looked at me. Then she walked away towards the graves with a small brazier of frankincense.

Alenush's face shone. "Can I invite him over?"

I looked at Martha, who was standing with her back to us.

"Why not?" I said.

Martha made the sign of the cross and kneeled by the first grave she came to.

Behzad said, "I'm only prejudiced against one thing: prejudice!"

Alenush laughed.

Martha said, "Would you like some more *ghormeh sabzi*?* Of course, it is not as tasty as the Persians' *ghormeh sabzi*."

Behzad said, "Persians? I'm not Persian. I'm a Turk – my father and mother are from Tabriz."

This made Alenush laugh even harder. "Armenians call all Iranians 'Persians,' no matter which part of Iran they're from."

I didn't know what was making me more uncomfortable: Martha's discomfort or Alenush and Behzad's lack of discomfort.

I said, "Behzad, do you play ping-pong?"

After lunch, Behzad and I played ping-pong. It had been years since I had played seriously. Even so, I won all three games.

Behzad put his racket down on the table. "I can't compete with you!"

Alenush laughed. "There are two things that no one can beat my dad at: ping-pong and…"

Behzad brushed away a lock of hair that had fallen onto Alenush's forehead. They looked at each other and smiled.

Martha asked, "Would you like some Turkish coffee?"

When it was time to go, I kissed my aunt on the cheek. Her face felt stiff, like Grandmother's cheek the last time I had kissed it as she lay on her enormous bed among the white sheets.

Auntie whispered in my ear, "Edmond, is everything all right? Martha isn't herself tonight."

I looked up and met Alenush's eyes. She was putting on her oversized coat, which reached to her ankles. She thrust her chin out and looked at me defiantly.

I put my hands on my aunt's shoulders. How frail she was. I said, "Yes, everything's fine. Martha is just a little tired these days."

My aunt nodded. "I understand. We're all a little tired these days."

Then she straightened my scarf. "Why don't you go to the North for a few days? You haven't been back for a long time, no?" And in my mind, I heard Danique's voice: *The textbooks are ready... in the North... we have nobody to bring them to Tehran...*

I nodded. "You're right. It has been a long time."

The following morning, when Alenush had gone out, Martha came out of the bedroom. I had made her coffee. She drank it and stood up. I stood next to the sink. Martha washed the cups and I dried them.

She said, "Why not? You can bring back the books, and you'll have a chance to talk to her, too."

The cup in my hand was certainly dry by now, so why was I still rubbing it with the dishtowel?

"You don't want to come?" I asked.

She shut off the tap, took off her rubber gloves, and hung them above the sink. Then she turned and looked at me. Just from last night to now, how much thinner she seemed!

She put her hand on my arm. "Edmond, I'm begging you. You have to do something about this."

My arm hurt where she gripped it. She released me and walked away. At the door of the kitchen she stopped to look at me again and said, "I just can't bear it." Her face was as white as the walls of the kitchen.

Alenush and I left for the North that afternoon. When we passed Karaj,* Alenush started to cry. It had been years since I had seen her cry. Even as a child she never cried much. I stopped at a café just at the beginning of the Chalus road. We sat down by the pool outside the café. Her eyes were still red.

She turned the small glass teacup around in its saucer. "You understand, don't you? You don't think I'm making a mistake?"

I held out my pack of cigarettes to her. She looked at me. I'd known for a long time that she smoked. I had never smoked in front of Grandmother, and even now I never smoked in front of my aunt. I lit her cigarette.

She puffed and exhaled the smoke. "Dad, I really love you, but I hope you didn't bring me along to try to give me a lecture."

When she had just started school, Martha had told her, "Girls must sit with their knees together." Alenush had stamped the ground and said, "Mom, spare me the lecture!"

She had pronounced "lecture" as "letcure" and Martha and I laughed.

Martha asked, "Alenush, what does 'letcure' mean?"

Alenush tossed her braids over her shoulder and said, "It means like when Grandmother and Auntie Shakeh talk."

Martha remonstrated, "Where are your manners?" and Alenush shrugged and left the room.

Alenush tapped her cigarette on the molded plastic ashtray. "What do you think of Behzad?"

The wind picked up the ash and blew it towards the statue of the angel that was in the middle of the pool.

On the cover of a book Behzad had brought me as a gift, there was a photo of a statue of an angel. Behzad said, "It's from an excavation of the temple of Anahita.* Isn't it beautiful?"

Martha said to me in Armenian, "It looks like the engraving on the altar in the St. Thaddeus Monastery.*"

Alenush translated for Behzad.

When I tried to pay for our tea, the café owner insisted that we must be his guests.

As we got back into the car, I said, "Of course you know that your mother and I have no problem with Behzad as a person."

Alenush leaned over, put her hands on the steering wheel, and stared at me. "You don't have a problem with him as a person! You just have a problem because of some medieval notions and traditions."

Ever since she first met Behzad, she had become more articulate not only in Persian, but also in Armenian.

I eased her hand off the steering wheel and looked at the road. "Alenush, spare me the lecture," I said.

We drove alongside the river, whose water was gray. I remembered it being other colors on other trips. Green and blue and brown. I wondered why its color should change every time. Once, on a trip to the North with my parents, Martha, and Alenush, the water had almost seemed orange.

My mother said, "It's the color of the leaves reflected in the water."

It had been fall then. That winter, Mother died, and Father the winter after.

The house seemed to have aged further since the last time we had visited. Wrinkled and faded, and older. The wooden rails on the upper balcony had collapsed here and there, the walls were cracked, and there was a musty smell everywhere. There was nowhere in the house that spiders hadn't colonized with their webs.

Alenush walked slowly through the house. "You can't even tell where they are."

"Who?" I asked.

"The spiders," she answered.

In my mother's room, she started to cry. "I wish you were still here," she whispered. "You would understand."

That night, we stayed in the town's old hotel.

In my younger days the owner of the hotel was a fat, bald Armenian man whose name was Aghajan. When I was a child, I was afraid of the big mole on his cheek. The hotel had no more than seven or eight rooms, but it had a very large reception room. All the ceremonies in our Armenian community, from weddings, baptisms, and New Year celebrations to the end-of-school year parties and memorial services, were held in that room. When I was ten or twelve years old, one night I slept over at the hotel. Our house was being painted and my mother, who was allergic to the smell of paint, insisted that we spend the night at the hotel.

Grandmother raised her eyebrows. "I've never heard such nonsense. You'll sleep at our house."

My aunt snorted. "What ridiculous excuses! You can stay with us, too."

My mother pressed her lips together, pushed her now short hair behind her ears, and stared at the ceiling.

Aghajan gave Mother and me the biggest room in the hotel, which had two brass beds, a carved wooden wardrobe and a mirror that covered half the wall. That night, my parents and I ate supper with Aghajan at a table next to the window looking out over the garden. Fenia was there, too. She was a blond Russian woman who always wore red lipstick and kissed the top of Aghajan's bald head in front of everyone. That night Mother laughed the whole evening. I was happy because she was happy, and because we were staying in a hotel, and focused my attention on slicing a lamb kebab that was hard to cut.

A piece of the kebab had leaped off my plate twice already when finally Fenia took the chop and picked the meat off the bones with her plump white fingers, then handed it back to me, saying, "Why are you making it so hard for yourself? Eat it this way! Isn't it easier?"

Aghajan chuckled. "That's why I love her. She always takes life easy."

My father laughed.

Mother laughed louder, and I remembered Grandmother and Auntie Shakeh talking about

Aghajan and Fenia, saying, "They'll answer for their sins in the next world."

That night I lay awake in the bronze bed of the hotel room for a while, watching my own shadow in the mirror and making up a story. I was a prince who had battled with four monsters to save a blond, blue-eyed princess. The monsters were the four high posts on the bed. The next morning on the way back to our house, Mother wiped off her red lipstick with a handkerchief.

I sat with Alenush at a table next to the window. The only things that hadn't changed from the old times were the orange trees in the garden. Here and there, the plaster ceiling of the reception room was falling down. The green velvet curtains were gone. The white cotton tablecloths were gone, too, and in their place were orange plastic ones.

I pointed to a corner of the room. "At New Year, they would put the Christmas tree over there."

A piece of kebab popped off Alenush's plate. She picked up the piece and put it in the ashtray. "Trees?" she asked absently. "Oh, right, they're pretty." And she looked out at the garden. Her profile reminded me of my mother.

We slept that night in two separate rooms. My room was small, with an iron bedstead and wardrobe. There was no mirror on the wall. I stayed awake for a while, thinking of my mother.

In my childhood, I had never thought twice about my mother having her own room, and I couldn't understand why it bothered other people so much.

One day, Grandmother and Auntie Shakeh were sitting at our kitchen table, drinking coffee with my other aunt, who was visiting. My mother wasn't home.

Auntie Shakeh said, "Everyone in town is talking about it."

My mother's sister said, "She's never cared about what other people think, not even when she was a child. She's always been stubborn. When we were kids, we hated meat stew. One day our father decreed that we had to eat it every day for lunch and dinner. My brother and I came around by the second day, but my sister went a whole week without eating until finally our father relented."

She laughed. Auntie and Grandmother shook their heads.

I said, "So what, I have my own room, why does it matter?"

"Who told you to listen to the grown-ups when they're talking?" my mother's sister snapped.

Grandmother sighed. "A woman must obey her husband."

Auntie Shakeh nodded.

Every time talk turned to my family, Alenush would say, "Your mother was the only open-minded person among you."

Martha would remonstrate, "Alenush, manners!" and Alenush would just laugh, as she did whenever she'd gotten her mother's goat.

I never understood why Grandmother loved Alenush more than all of her other grandchildren and their offspring. Every time we were due to visit Grandmother, Alenush would come up with a host of excuses not to go. Martha or I would say, "But your great-grandmother loves you so much," and she would stamp her foot and say, "I can't stand her house! Don't you get it? There's nothing to play with. You can't touch anything. The curtains are all dark and heavy and the lights are dim. It's depressing. Why don't you understand?" We could only bring her around by promising to "only stay a short time and to visit Mamali's house afterward."

"Mamali" was my mother. As soon as Alenush saw Mamali she would rush to clasp her arms around her neck and kiss her, saying, "You smell so good! I love it here. It's so full of light. It's wonderful!"

At my mother's house, Alenush had permission to play all of her odd games and was free to do anything she liked. The day she poured an expensive bottle of my mother's perfume down the drain in the bathroom, Martha had wanted to punish her, but Mother just laughed so hard the tears rolled down her face. "How wonderful! Now for two or three weeks the bathroom will smell lovely." Then, as Martha stared in amazement and I tried not to laugh, grandmother and granddaughter giggled together as though they'd die of amusement.

Another time Martha and I had left Alenush with my mother while we went to do some shopping, and when we got back, Alenush was sitting in the middle of the living room. On either side of her were two antique china vases, and she was ladling sugar from one to the other. My mother sat on an armchair, reading a book.

Martha yelled, "Nunush! What are you doing? You'll break them."

My mother closed her book. "Oh, let them break. They're of no use to me."

The vases were a gift from Grandmother, I couldn't remember for which occasion.

Martha, either out of her own concern or because she was taken aback by Mother's lack of concern, protested, "But the room is full of ants!"

Alenush clapped her hands together. "Hurray! Now we can have a tea party with the ants. Will you play, too?" She looked at my mother.

Mother bent over and inspected the line of ants that was carrying away the grains of sugar. Then she got up from her chair, sat cross-legged on the floor, and said, "The ants on this side are mine, the ones on that side are yours."

Martha frowned all evening and wouldn't speak to me because I had started laughing.

That night in the hotel room, I thought of Aghajan and Fenia, and wondered what kind of answer they'd gotten in the next world.

The next morning the beach was quiet, full of seashells and seaweed. We walked and talked. Mostly Alenush talked. I listened and thought about how carefully she chose her words. We sat down on the big rocks and tree trunks, and when it was my turn to talk, my words sounded bookish and repetitive to my own ears.

When I was a child, I would try to listen carefully to the priest in church. Sometimes when I didn't understand a word he had used, I would ask Grandmother about it. Grandmother would say,

"There is no need to understand every word the priest says. As long as we know that he never says anything untrue, and we think about God and Jesus when we are in church, that is enough."

Alenush looked out at the sea, chin in hand. She took a cigarette out of my pack and lit it. On the way back, my hand was on my daughter's shoulder.

On our last afternoon before we moved to Tehran for good, my mother and I went down to the beach. I was carrying a big bag full of all the seashells and stones that I had collected over the years.

The day before, Father had thrown a fit. "We'll need a separate truck for all of your junk. Throw it out!"

Mother was walking a few steps ahead of me. She was crying.

I sat on a tree stump and emptied out the bag. I looked at the pile that had formed next to me, then at my mother, who was getting further and further away, then back at the pile on the sand. I picked up the stones one by one. I remembered when and where I had found each of them. This round one that looked like a pig's snout, I had found the day my father took me boar-hunting.

Arsham and my uncle and father were spread out on top of a small hill and scouting around them. I was at the bottom of the hill with my back to them, staring at the ground. I closed my eyes and put my hands over my ears so that I would not hear the shots, and the first thing I saw when I opened my eyes was this stone. For ten days my father showed everyone the stone and said, "This is what Edmond caught hunting!" and for the hundredth time I regretted showing my father something that I cared about.

The seashells were from the times when Tahereh, the school janitor's daughter, and I had competed to see who could collect more. Tahereh got tired of the game fast. "There's seashells from here to tomorrow. Come on, let's try to find something there's not so much of."

"Like what?" I asked.

She flipped her braids over her shoulder, stared straight ahead for a few moments, then said, "Like a black stone with a blue streak."

I tried so hard to find a stone like that! Then one day at school, Tahereh put her hand in the pocket of her uniform and said, "Look! I found it. I don't want to play anymore." And she gave me the stone.

A few days later when I was playing with my stones and seashells, I ran my hand over the stone and the blue streak came off. When I said to Tahereh, "You cheated, that's not fair," she widened her eyes and started to giggle.

I spread out my seashells and stones with a branch. Then one by one I threw them into the sea. Mother was walking back towards me. I threw the branch out as far as I could.

Mother put her hand on my shoulder. "Shall we go back?"

I put the black stone without a blue streak in my pocket.

On the way back to the hotel, Alenush and I passed by Mrs. Grigorian's sherbet shop. For the umpteenth time, I was astonished to find her still alive. Pasted on the dusty window of the shop was a cardboard sign and printed on it in Armenian and Persian was: *Turkish coffee – Hot chocolate – Tea.*

Alenush said, "Shall we have a coffee?"

Mrs. Grigorian was sitting behind a table in the shop, breaking up bits of bread.

After I had gone through all of my explanation about who we were and how we used to live here, she said, "I don't remember. Since my dear brother died, I haven't been able to remember much."

Alenush asked, "Why are you tearing up that bread?"

Mrs. Grigorian answered, "For the pigeons. My

dear brother was the first person here to open a sherbet shop. Did you say you wanted coffee?"

She stood up and went to the kitchen in the back of the shop.

Alenush sat at the table.

I looked around the shop. It hadn't changed much. The same wooden counter, the same rickety wooden chairs, the same wall hangings. It was just that it seemed smaller now…and where was the sherbet machine? I poked my head behind the counter. My guess was correct. Dusty and faded, it had fallen in the middle of a nest of newspapers and magazines and junk. One of its glass urns was broken. When I was a child I had dreamed again and again of the two-headed eagles etched on its sides. Alenush said, "What are you looking at?"

I showed her the machine. "It would make three kinds of sherbet: orange, lemon, and sour cherry. I never liked the taste of any of them."

Mrs. Grigorian brought a little tray with two mismatched demitasse cups on it and set it on the table. "Alvart was my best friend. Such a pure soul! There's no one else like her."

Alenush poked me. "Tell her she was your grandmother!"

I tried.

Mrs. Grigorian nodded. "Every day in the morning they call out from the roof, waiting for their crumbs. Only the pigeons are left for me now. My little friends."

Alenush broke up bread quietly for a few minutes. When it was time to go, she leaned down to kiss the old woman.

As we left the shop, she said, "Her face felt like stone."

She took a Kleenex out of her backpack and wiped her eyes.

We rang the bell, knocked on the door and shouted until someone finally opened the door. The church watchman was a small man wearing a hearing aid. A couple of the buttons on his checkered coat were missing.

When I introduced myself, he said, "Of course I remember you. I was in the same class as your cousin. Our classroom was over there."

I looked at the school. In front of the classrooms on the ground floor, there were large spindles one after another.

The watchman fiddled with his hearing aid. "A few years ago the school became a Tricot workshop. Mrs. Grigorian wouldn't allow them to use the church courtyard to come and go. So they opened a door from the street. Do you want me to open up the church? Ever since the church was robbed, I've been keeping it locked. I only open it on All Saints' Day. The missus burns incense over all the graves every year. Last year…"

I looked at the middle room on the ground floor where in those days the school janitor and his family had lived. Its door was wide open. A young man in an undershirt was pushing the handle of a machine right and left.

Alenush walked among the tall trees and the weeds and read out the inscriptions on the gravestones. "These people aren't related to us at all. Why did Mother burn incense for them?"

I stood next to the statue of the merchant's wife.

Alenush put her hand on the statue's bare shoulder. She picked a piece of moss out of her hair. "Poor thing."

"Poor thing?" I repeated.

She walked around the statue. "Auntie Shakeh told me her story."

She ran a hand over the stone shawl. Then all of a sudden she turned and stared at me. "She figured a way to sort out her problem, right?"

My heart sank. I had never contemplated being separated from my daughter.

I remembered lying in my bed and listening to the shouting from the living room next door.

"I don't want to! I didn't want to get married to begin with. My father forced me into it. If it wasn't for the child, I would have left already. It's for his sake that I endure this. If you bring up my room again, I swear to God I'm leaving!"

My father's voice shook. "Are you threatening me? No one is keeping you here. The door is open – you can walk right through it."

Grandmother shouted, "Stop it! There have never been such things in our family. You must compromise."

"God Almighty! Have mercy on us," Auntie Shakeh repeated a few times.

I put my head under my pillow and cried. My heart sank. I had never imagined I could be separated from my mother.

All the way back, Alenush talked. She talked about her classes and her professors and the university. About the Turkmen dances she had seen a few weeks ago. She said she was thinking about sewing herself a Turkmen costume. Outside the little printing shop she helped me load the textbooks into the trunk of the car. They were Armenian-language books for first-to-third graders.

When we got back on the road, she picked up one of the first-grade books and began to read. "Do you remember how hard it was for me to write the letter 'F'?" she asked. I remembered.

"Do you remember how I would blacken in the center of all the 'O's?"

I remembered.

"Do you remember when I memorized the poem, 'The Green Plains of My Homeland'? You bought me a pencil holder as a reward."

I remembered.

She closed the book. She looked at the road and said, "The first poem I ever memorized was 'The Golden Fish.' I wasn't even in school yet. Mamali taught it to me."

She began to recite the poem. I recited it along with her.

We drank tea in the same coffee house, next to the same pool with its angel statue. The owner once again insisted that we be his guests.

When we got back into the car, Alenush laughed. "What do you think he would do if we took him seriously and didn't pay?" She began to sing an old Armenian song.

I looked at the river. The water seemed green.

PART III

white violets

Tomorrow it will be Easter.

I arrange the white wool bedspread, knitted by my grandmother, on the double bed. It's made up of small squares of different patterns sewn together. I can't remember when Grandmother made this bedspread, or for which birthday or anniversary she had given it as a gift to Martha.

Though there were many brides who came to our family over the years, Grandmother and Auntie Shakeh would only give gifts of their knitting and embroidery to Martha. Grandmother and Auntie used to say, "Only Martha understands their true value."

I come out of the bedroom. My slippers make a muffled sound on the stairs. I look at them. The buckle on the left one is coming loose and the gray leather on their tops is turning white.

A few days ago Danique came to see me, and when she looked at my slippers, she said, "These guys are through with you. Why aren't you through with them?"

I've known for quite a while now that I should throw them away, but somehow I just can't. It was Martha who always bought my slippers, like all my other personal things: my shaving cream, my *Eau Sauvage* cologne and, after Mother died, the green ink for my fountain pen.

It was my mother who bought me green ink for the first time, along with the fountain pen she gave me as a gift to mark my graduation from high school.

When I asked, "Why green?" she laughed and shrugged. "I don't know, maybe just because it's different from black and blue."

My father smirked. "'It's different from black and blue!' Madam insists that all of her things be different from those of other people."

My mother looked at him for a few moments and then turned to me. Nowadays, she had to look up at me to meet my eyes, and I had to lean down to kiss her. She said, "Write something, see if you like it."

On the corner of the *Alik** newspaper that was delivered to our house in the afternoons for my father, I wrote, "Green ink is different from all other inks. I like people and things that are different."

Mother laughed. Father looked at us for a minute, then snatched the newspaper off the table and left the room.

Mother shook her head calmly. "He never understands."

From that day until the day she died, it was Mother's job to buy green ink for my pen.

One afternoon soon after we were married, Martha and I were sitting with my mother in the courtyard of our house drinking tea. I said to my mother, "I'm out of ink."

"Why are you bothering your mother?" Martha asked. "I'll buy it."

My mother put a hand on Martha's arm. "Will you allow me?" Then she laughed awkwardly and ran her hand over her skirt again and again as though she were trying to wipe something off it. "I never did anything for Edmond when he was a child. From the time he was little, he took care of himself. In the mornings he would get himself up, make his own breakfast, and see himself off to school. He'd put breakfast on the table for me, too."

Martha turned and looked at me uncomfortably, then stood up. "More tea?" she asked, and I remembered the breakfasts that I used to make.

Those early mornings were the best part of my day. The house was quiet and you could hear the incessant chirping of the sparrows that flitted about in the branches of the orange trees in the garden. I left my room, opened Mother's door quietly and poked my head in. I liked to watch her sleep. She always slept on her stomach, hugging the pillow. Sometimes she smiled in her sleep. I thought she must be having a good dream. In the afternoon when I'd ask, "What did you dream about last night?" she would narrow her eyes and say, "I dreamed of a little boy who poked his head into my room." "Oh come on!" I'd say. "Really, what did you dream about?" and Mother would describe her dreams to me. It seemed as though she was always running in a huge desert or flying above a jungle. When I got older, I thought she must have had bad dreams, too. But she never told me about those.

In the early morning the kitchen was all mine. I made tea, laid out the breakfast things, and all the time I talked to myself. Sometimes I was myself, sometimes someone else. My father, my mother, my teachers, my aunt, my grandmother. My morning people were the way I liked them to be. Father was polite and kind, Mother laughed more, my teachers weren't so strict, Auntie Shakeh and Grandmother liked my mother, and I always had the right answers to give people, which I could never manage in real life. Breakfast finished, I'd gather up the bread-crumbs on my plate and scatter them on the kitchen windowsill. In a minute, the pigeons would arrive. I knew each of them and had names for them all:

"Grumpy," "Dotty," Fatty," and "Grand Dame." When they had finished eating the crumbs, they would cock their heads and look at me, as though waiting for more. Some days, Mother woke up early and came into the kitchen, and we played tea party. I would pour her tea and put it in front of her and say, "Here you are, madam." She would bow her head and say, "Thank you, sir, forgive me for attending your table without having brushed my hair." Or when she was still sleepy, she would stare at the sugar bowl or at the cup of tea, and I liked to watch her. If it took too long for her to snap out of it, I would pass my hand in front of her face and say, "Hellloooo...hellooooo," and she would laugh. I could never decide which I liked better: my mornings with my mother or with my pigeons.

I go to the kitchen. The coffee pot is in its usual place, hanging from a hook above the sink. I pull a teaspoon out of a drawer on the right, and sugar and Turkish coffee from the cupboard above. I measure out what's needed: one spoonful of sugar, one spoonful of coffee, one not-quite-full cup of water.

After four years I still can't get myself together. Sometimes when I sink into the silence of the house, or glance at a photograph that brings back distant memories, I fall back into my old habits of twenty-odd years and make two cups of coffee. It's always painful to empty the second cup out into the sink.

A few days ago when I poured a cup of coffee for myself and saw that there was still coffee left in the pot, I took down the pink coffee cup with its broken handle and filled it. Martha always drank her coffee from that cup. I took the cups to the sitting room and put them on the little side table between the two armchairs. Martha and I sat here every morning and drank our coffee. I sat down in my usual place in front of the window and drank my coffee. I looked out at the garden and talked in a loud voice with the full, handle-less cup of coffee.

I had bought the set of pink coffee cups in one of the shops near the Qavam al-Saltaneh* intersection, and brought them home along with the news that I'd been promoted to school principal. Alenush wasn't even born yet.

The years passed and the cups broke one by one until the only one left was this handle-less, saucerless cup. Martha would laugh and say, "This last one is my cup of life! If it breaks, that's the end of me!" And now…

I sit in my usual place in the sitting room and look out at the garden. A few sparrows are disporting themselves in the dry and cracked earth of the flower bed, flitting about here and there. If they are the same sparrows of years past, do they ask each other why no one has planted violets these past few years? Maybe they aren't even the same sparrows, though; or maybe they are and they've gotten used to a garden without violets. So why can't I?

I drink my coffee, light a cigarette, and try to remember all the different kinds of violets that Martha planted for Easter in the garden over twenty-odd years. How many violets had she planted? Ten thousand? Twenty thousand? A small mountain of violets. The phone rings.

As always, Danique's voice is cheerful and concerned. "What are you up to?"

"I'm having coffee. What are you doing?"

"Making *kuku sabzi*." She laughs.

Danique's clumsiness in the kitchen is an old story. Martha always teased her. "They should put your name in the history books. The first Armenian woman who doesn't know how to cook!"

Alenush hugged Danique and kissed her. "Don't be sad, Auntie Danique. I've decided never to learn how to cook so that you won't be lonely."

Martha rolled her eyes and said, "God help us!" and all three laughed.

Danique says, "Please don't be late, because if you are, I'll blame the burnt *kuku* and the mushy rice on you! I'm already blaming the saltiness of the smoked fish on the fish merchant. Eight o'clock sharp."

"Eight o'clock sharp," I promise.

I return to the sitting room. For the second year I'll be Danique's guest for Easter dinner.

My cousin Arsham, along with the rest of my extended family, moved abroad years ago. Auntie has been one of the "eternal sleepers" for some years now, and it's been four years since Martha…

Now I understand why Grandmother didn't like to talk directly about death.

Every Sunday I take a bouquet of flowers to the cemetery. On each grave, I place a flower: Grandmother, Father, Mother, Auntie Shakeh. The rest of the flowers are for Martha. Sometimes Danique comes with me. When we get to Martha's grave, she stands next to me for a few moments. Sometimes she helps me clean the grave, or sits next to me for a while, then gets up. I see her walking among the graves and reading the stones, or disappearing behind the church. Sometimes she goes into the church; I can't see that well from where I'm sitting. *How alone she is*, I think. *Why doesn't she take care of herself? Haven't all these years of penance been enough?* I light a little piece of frankincense in a vase and say to myself, *That episode was so many years ago. Why can't I talk to her about it now? I must do something to set her free from her solitude. It's still not too late.* Then I remember what Martha used to say. "Be patient, she'll tell you herself."

Danique returns just as I am finishing my inner dialogue with Martha and have arranged and rearranged the flowers on her grave several times. Her eyes are red. I think, *I wish she would talk about it.*

The whole thing began when the school board decided to retire Adamian. Breaking the news to him fell to me. I knew that it wasn't going to be easy. Martha said, "He'll think this is Danique's doing."

Danique had been working in the school for a few months by then, but right from the beginning, Adamian hadn't got along with her. This wasn't surprising. Adamian didn't get along with anyone. Not with the teachers, not with the children's parents, and not with the students. He only tolerated me, and that was because I tolerated him.

Martha was right. Adamian didn't accept that at the age of sixty-five, after forty years of service, it was time to retire, nor that this wasn't the consequence of scheming and subterfuge. He saw it all as Danique's doing and when he started to complain about Danique and, as always, I stopped him, he got up, stood facing me, put his hands on my desk and said, "Sir, I am sorry that you prefer an immodest, disreputable woman to an honest employee."

I felt my chest tighten.

I remembered a day when my mother and I were returning from shopping. It was around the time that school was about to start. We had bought a new schoolbag, new shoes, and pink and blue wrapping paper to cover my textbooks.

When we left the shop I said to my mother, "Do you think the shop owner was telling the truth when he said that in the wrapping-paper factory they roll out all kinds of paper on the floor so that he can walk on them and choose what he wants?"

My mother laughed. "Why would he lie?"

I held my mother's hand in one hand and the roll of colored wrapping paper in the other. I was thinking how wonderful it would be to walk over such beautiful paper, when suddenly my mother screamed.

A thin, young man had just brushed past her, and grabbed her breast. The schoolbag and box of shoes fell out of my mother's hands as she covered her chest. The young man laughed and ran off. My mother started to cry.

A lady passing by stopped, bent down, picked up the packages, and handed them back to my mother. "Shame on them!" she said. "As if they don't have mothers or sisters of their own."

A man, who was standing in front of a shop with his hands in his pockets, grinned.

My mother handed me the packages, straightened the torn collar of her dress with both hands, and cried all the way home. How I loved that dress. It had a lace collar and small pearl buttons from the neck to the waist. We got home, and Mother was crying even harder. When Father heard about the incident, he continued leafing through his newspaper and said, "If you don't want to be harassed in the street, don't wear such provocative dresses." I went to my room, spread out the wrapping paper, and stamped on it again and again until it was in shreds.

Adamian was still talking and I was tearing a piece of paper on my desk into little shreds.

"Sir, I've been trying to talk to you about this for a while, but you wouldn't let me. Now if you will allow me…"

He sat, as was his habit, bolt upright. "You know that I am from Tabriz." I knew. "And you know that this woman also came to Tehran from Tabriz."

On the day of her interview, Danique had said, "I was born in Tabriz but I've decided to live in Tehran." She didn't say more than that. Later I asked Martha several times why Danique's family never came to visit her in Tehran, or why she herself never went to Tabriz, but Martha either changed the subject or simply stayed silent. I knew that this meant that she didn't want to talk about it.

Adamian began again. He had been suspicious of Danique right from the beginning. He had written a letter to his relatives in Tabriz, asking them to look into Danique's past. Their reply had come a month ago. There was no need for a detailed investigation: every Armenian in Tabriz knew Danique's story.

The words "disreputable" and "immodest" whirled around in my head. One day, at my grandmother's, she had said, "A respectable woman obeys her father until the day she marries, and after holy matrimony, she must submit to her husband. This has been our tradition and custom for thousands of years."

My mother snorted. "Oh? And what do our thousand years of tradition say about men's respectability?"

Adamian's soft voice and confidential tone bothered me more than usual. "She was in love with their Muslim neighbor." There was a large boil on Adamian's cheek. "Without a thought for her family's feelings on the matter, she insisted she wanted to marry this boy!" Adamian's left eyelid twitched. "Shamed by the public humiliation, her poor mother became sick, and this madam, after all the trouble she'd caused, left for Tehran."

Adamian raised his head, looked at me, and smiled crookedly. His face had the same triumphant expression whenever he was punishing a student for not bringing his notebook or textbook, or for laughing too loudly in the schoolyard.

Maybe he was waiting for me to call Danique to my office right there and then and fire her. When I said, "We aren't interested in employees' private affairs," he went white, jumped up, and walked over to the door. As he put his hand on the knob, I said, "By the way, has your daughter-in-law had the cast removed from her arm yet?"

He slammed the door. A few months earlier, Adamian's son had beaten his wife so badly that her arm had been broken in three places.

That night at dinner, I related the story to Martha. She started breaking off bits of bread and rolling it into little balls, and didn't say anything for a while.

"I wish you had told me," I said. "If I had known…"

Martha shook her head. "Hasn't the poor thing suffered enough in Tabriz? And now this? Why won't they leave her alone?"

She started to gather up the dishes. "Think of what they've done to her. They beat her! The priest excommunicated her in front of the whole congregation. Children and adults spat in her face in the street." Her voice was trembling. "Her cousin wanted to kill her!"

She put the dishes in the sink and turned to me. "Just imagine. They said to her, 'What, aren't we good enough for you?'"

I had never seen Martha so angry. As I took her hands, she laid her head on my shoulder and started to cry. "Edmond, help her! Please."

The next day at the board meeting, I argued her case for hours.

On my way back home, I thought to myself, *Why am I defending Danique? For my sake? For her sake? For*

Martha's sake? Wasn't the way Martha behaved last night strange? Did that mean she loved Danique so much that she was willing to forgive her that mistake? It wasn't a mistake: for Martha, what Danique did was a sin! But was it just a mistake? Was it a sin? Wasn't it? I felt dizzy.

When we had put Alenush to bed, Martha and I discussed it. She sat quietly for a few minutes. Then she said, "I know. I've thought about it a lot myself…I don't know. Maybe because I like her so much, maybe because I know that she's not a frivolous woman. Maybe because everyone makes mistakes sometimes…" Then she looked at me and said, "Edmond, falling in love isn't a sin, is it?"

Two days later, in Adamian's presence, I named Danique the school's new vice-principal. Adamian left without saying so much as goodbye. At Martha's request, I never said a word to Danique about what had happened. Martha said, "Let her tell you herself." But Danique never did tell me.

On the Sundays when Danique comes with me to the cemetery, she sits next to me, runs a hand over the gravestone and talks to me about Martha. About little things she remembers: small, sweet memories, like the day they went to buy fabric together and

Danique convinced Martha to buy a white cloth patterned with red polka dots instead of a boring brown one. When Alenush saw her mother wearing the dress made out of the new fabric, and with short sleeves to boot, she said, "You look so pretty. Just like a lollipop."

I remembered that dress with the short sleeves well. Anytime we wanted to go somewhere, Alenush would say to Martha, "Wear the lollipop dress!"

Sitting next to Martha's grave, I look at Danique and think to myself, *I have to bring it up. Tomorrow or the day after tomorrow, or maybe even today on the way home.*

On the way home, I'm numb and tired. The road is monotonous and slow, and all I can do is think to myself, *What is it I'm going home to? Who's waiting for me there? What am I waiting for? Maybe the occasional letter from Alenush.* When I get home, I make myself a cup of coffee, read a book, eat something, iron my shirts, go through the motions of living, and say to myself, *Tomorrow. Tomorrow I must speak to Danique.*

The sparrows are still flitting about in the dirt in the flower bed, this way and that. What am I going to do until eight o'clock? Should I go for a walk for a few hours? It's not a bad idea. I get up and take my coffee cup to the kitchen. I wash it, dry it, and put it in the cupboard.

I remember to take the house key with me. Martha used to say, "If I weren't here to open it, you'd be left standing outside the door each day!" I say to myself, *Now that you aren't here, I remember the key.*

Mohammad, the son of Ali who owns the grocery shop at the top of our lane, says hello to me. "How's it going, sir? You look a bit tired."

I return his greeting. What have I done to make myself so tired? For some time now, I haven't left the house much. Since Martha has been gone, Danique has been principal of the school in everything but name. In the morning I call her. "Everything okay? Do you need me for anything?"

Her laugh rings out through the receiver. "Everything's okay!"

Then sometimes, on the same day, or sometimes the next morning, she will call me. "Edmond, please come straightaway. Something's come up. You need to be here."

I know that I don't need to be there. I know that Danique can handle anything. I know that she only wants to ensure that my ties to the outside world, already fragile, don't further fray, and then I feel tired. So tired.

I talk with Mohammad for a while and remember that he has gotten married and I still have not bought him a gift.

Martha used to give gifts to everyone in the neighborhood – neighbor or shopkeeper, Christian or Muslim – for every occasion, be it a birthday, wedding, or coming first at school. At Easter, all the children in the neighborhood would gather at our house to receive colored eggs from "Mrs. Principal." For our New Year, Martha would make *nazouk* pastries and send them to Ali's wife and all of the other neighbors. And in return, Ali's wife would send us chickpea cookies for Norouz.*

Alenush loved chickpea cookies. She would pick them up one after the other, pop them in her mouth, close her eyes, and say, "Mmmmm…delicious!"

Martha and Ali's wife would always praise each other's baking. "Your *nazok* is indescribable, Mrs. Principal."

Martha laughed. "It's not *nazok*, it's *nazouk*! And by the way, they're nothing as good as your chickpea cookies."

And Ali's wife, chubby and rosy-cheeked, would pull her flowered *chador* back up over her head and laugh softly. "Oh, they're not so special," she'd say.

During the month of Muharram* our house

would fill with bowls of *sholeh zard**pudding. Alenush, Martha, and all of the family loved *sholeh zard*. Once, Martha got the recipe from Ali's wife and tried to make it. Alenush tasted it and said, "Ummm... nope." Martha tasted it herself. "Nope!" and laughed. "Everyone has something they're good at."

I say goodbye to Mohammad, wondering what sort of wedding gift I should buy for him. If only Martha were here – she would know for sure what to get. She would have told me at lunch or dinner or breakfast, "Mohammad got married. I bought him a gift." And of course I would only have nodded and forgotten the next moment what she had bought for Mohammad.

On the main street near our lane, there is a piece of land that has never been developed. It is right between Mr. Maleki's carpentry shop and Mr. Harootunian's confectionery. Martha, when she wanted to give directions to our house, would say, "It's the lane next to the dump."

One year in the spring a dog gave birth to eight puppies there. Alenush had just started going to school, and the first time she saw the puppies she insisted, "We have to take them home with us. They'll die of cold here."

"Absolutely not!" Martha said.

Alenush cried and stamped her feet and refused to eat.

The puppies became the most important issue in our household and for everyone in the neighborhood. Finally Mr. Maleki promised to build a kennel for the dogs.

Each morning Alenush would go out with a bag of leftovers. We would stop to pick up the two bottles of milk that Ali never charged us for and along with Mohammad, who was waiting for us, we'd set off to see the dogs.

I'd have to repeat, "Kids, you're going to be late for school," several times before they could tear themselves away. Mohammad and Alenush renamed the dump "the doghouse."

Even now, when Ali wants to give someone directions, he says, "after the doghouse," or "before you get to the doghouse," and if they aren't familiar with the neighborhood and look at him strangely, he laughs and says, "I mean the dump next to the confectionery."

When I get to the dump, I stand and look. It is full of flowerpots. Sweet briar and roses and box trees and oleanders. Little cedar saplings, nasturtiums planted in old cooking-oil tins, boxes of snapdragons, violets, and gillyflowers. Mr. Maleki, the carpenter, has a pencil behind one ear and his shirt is coming untucked as always. He is talking to a young man, but when he sees me, he scratches the back of his neck, then calls over, "You see this, Principal? The doghouse has become a hothouse!"

The young man, who seems to feel that I need an explanation, says, "I got permission from the city council."

He doesn't have a Tehran accent. I watch the flowers swaying back and forth in the wind. They're so colorful!

I ask, "Where are you from?" and gaze at the violets.

As if this question has reassured him, he bends over to pick up a few empty flowerpots and begins to stack them. "I'm from Lorestan."

I stare at the violets again. All four boxes are white. "What a lovely place. Why would you leave it and come to Tehran? Don't you miss it?"

He arranges a few boxes of ivy. "You can be sorry to the end of the day, you know, but what good is a beautiful place if you can't make ends meet? Right?"

A pickup truck full of lumber parks nearby and someone calls to Mr. Maleki. I notice something red on one of the violets and bend over to take a closer look.

The young man wipes his muddy hands on his wide trousers. "They're the first violets of spring, mister. Take some."

A ladybug is basking in the sun on the white petal of a violet.

I close my eyes. Then I open them. "How much for a box?" I ask.

All afternoon, Hushang and I plant the violets in my garden.

By the time the flower beds are full of violets, I know that Hushang is twenty-three years old. He's been in Tehran for two years. His father is dead. His mother and four sisters live in one of the villages near Khorramabad.* A suitor has asked for one of his sisters' hands, and Hushang is in love with the girl who lives next door. The girl next door is in love with the idea of living in Tehran.

When I pay him for his labor, Hushang hands me a flowerpot as a gift. "It's oregano. Dry it and sprinkle it on kebab, it's delicious. Really tasty. Your missus knows how to make kebab, right?"

I shake hands with Hushang and close the door.

It's almost seven o'clock. I wash my hands and face and change my clothes. Danique had said, "Eight o'clock! Don't be late." The white violets look as though they haven't quite gotten used to their new home yet.

I leave the house. It's not far to Danique's, and I decide to walk. Mr. Ali is unpacking boxes of soda in his shop. How white his hair has become! I remember the day that he came to our house to talk with Martha and me. He took off his hat, and I thought, *What thick, black hair he has.* When he left, Martha said, "What a sensible, intelligent man."

That night when Alenush got home, she heard the story and giggled. "What? Me and Mohammad?"

Martha, sitting at the dinner table, pointed a finger at her. "Listen to me, Nunush. Mr. Ali didn't come here for your hand in marriage. This poor man is more intelligent than anyone knows. He wants you to explain things to Mohammad, and you're going to! You're going to do it, and you're going to do it right. God help you if I find out that you've made fun of this poor boy. Understand?"

Alenush lowered her head and said, "Yes, Mother."

From then on, one of Martha's favorite expressions was, "You don't need a degree to have common sense!"

Danique's house is as it ever was: small, tidy, humid, and full of flowerpots great and small.

Every time we went to Danique's house, Martha would say, "It's the Amazon jungle in here! What's the name of this one?"

Danique's laughter rang out in the tiny sitting room. "Umbrella palm. It needs a lot of water to live, and humidity."

Martha loved maidenhair ferns. Danique brought her a few pots every year as a gift, but they always dried up and died. Danique's ferns were always healthy, with shiny green leaves and black stalks, which Alenush said looked like power cords.

Martha would say, "They're the prettiest plants in the world! Why is it so hard to keep them alive?"

Alenush pulled a face. "Taking care of beautiful things isn't easy – it's like taking care of me!"

Martha rolled her eyes. "Good grief, a fraction of this wit would be sufficient." We laughed and I remembered the ferns that grew higgledy-piggledy everywhere in the spring in the coastal town where I had grown up. Who had looked after them? No one even paid attention to them. No one, except maybe me and Tahereh, who walked through the courtyard of the school and the graveyard, looking for them and counting them.

Danique's dinner table is impeccable: it's laid with a white cotton cloth, matching napkins, two candlesticks with tall candles, and, as always, a small maidenhair fern set in a pot in the middle. Danique brings out the dinner and says, "I'm so sorry, I didn't have time to go get the holy wafer." I know not having time is just an excuse for not going to the church to get it. Martha and Danique's arguments over going or not going to church were endless.

One Sunday Martha said to Alenush, "You can't go to church in pants!" Alenush was only eight or nine years old then, but she put her hand on her hip and said, "Fine! Then I'm not going. I'm going to Auntie Danique's."

Martha looked at me helplessly.

I said, "Auntie Danique is coming with us to church."

Alenush looked at me. "Oh, really? Since when does she go to church?"

Martha bit her bottom lip. "What a mouth on this girl!" and went to the telephone. After half an hour the doorbell rang. It was Danique, wearing a brown suit and with a white scarf on her head.

Alenush jumped into her arms and said, "Auntie, shall we go for a walk?" Danique looked at Martha and winked. "Of course! After church we'll go to

Naderi Street* for *pierogis*. Now hurry up and put
on your pleated blue skirt and a white shirt."

Off she ran to change her clothes. Martha gave
a sigh of relief. Alenush loved the jam-filled *pierogis*
at Khosravi's on Naderi Street.

We eat dinner and talk. We talk about school,
about the teachers and the students. Then talk
turns to Alenush. Danique asks, "Have you had a
letter lately?"

I shake my head.

"She sent me an Easter card. Do you want to
see it?"

She gets up. In a corner of the room on a round
table, there must be more than twenty greeting cards,
large and small. She picks one up and hands it to
me. "While you're reading it, I'll get the tea ready,"
she says, and heads into the kitchen.

On the front of the card are a few bunnies hold-
ing out big colored eggs. Over the bunnies' heads
a message is written in English: "For the best aunt
in the world." Martha, like me, didn't have any
siblings. Alenush used to say, "Thank goodness for
Danique. If it weren't for her, I'd have no one to
call 'auntie.'"

After all these years, I still don't know if Danique herself has any brothers or sisters. I should ask when she brings out the tea. It's a good way to start talking about what I want to talk about. I open the card. *Dear Aunt Dottie…*

I get up and put the card back in its place on the table, next to the others. I wonder who sent all these cards. Probably students from the school. All of the students love Danique.

Danique brings in the tea tray and sets it on the table. "Did you read it?"

She sits. She puts a cup of tea in front of me. Then she puts her own in front of herself. First mine: two and a half teaspoons of sugar. Then hers: one neat teaspoon. I stir my tea and say to myself that when she's stirred hers, too, I'll begin. Danique stirs her tea. Then suddenly she says, "Edmond, how long do you think you can go on this way?"

My spoon sits motionless in my cup.

"Isn't four years enough? Four years of you being tormented here and Alenush suffering on the other side of the world?"

I look at the steam rising from the tea. *What does she mean? Why does she think I am torturing myself? How is Alenush being harmed? Alenush has been leading her own life for many years now. She seems to be satisfied with it. Sometimes she writes me a letter. I answer them. What more can I do?*

Danique folds her hands in her lap. "This poor girl almost died from suffering waiting for Martha to finally reconcile herself to the situation, and now you…"

After Alenush left Iran, Danique came to our house almost every day to sit with Martha in her room. When we were all three together, we didn't speak of Alenush. I felt that when Danique was alone with me, she was uncomfortable. At first I didn't understand why. Then one day I asked Martha, "Where is my red tie?"

Martha said, "It's not in the closet? Where it always is?"

The tie was right in front of me.

Martha asked, "Did you find it?"

I looked at the tie in my hand for a few moments. Then I said, "I found it. By the way, could you tell Danique that unless she wants me to, I'm not going to bring it up?"

When two years had passed since Alenush left, a letter came one morning. Martha, without looking at me, asked, "What sort of wedding gift do you think we should buy for our daughter?"

Danique smoothes the tablecloth with one hand. "Four years of penance isn't enough for Alenush?"

I lower my head, but I know that she's looking at me. "Edmond. Martha's death happened! It's not fair to blame Alenush."

My mouth is dry. The teaspoon shakes in my hand. *Why did she bring it up? I don't talk about it with anyone. I don't even allow myself to think about it. I know it's not fair. But it's out of my hands.*

It was early morning. Martha had been talking with someone on the phone for a quarter of an hour. When she put the receiver back in the cradle and came to the sitting room, I could guess what she had been talking about.

She sat down in the armchair facing the garden and said, "How many times do we have to explain? If only she were here herself! She could tell everyone off. I can't do it."

I put a cup of coffee in front of her and didn't ask who had been on the phone. What difference did it make? It had been more than two years since Alenush left, and by now we had become used to telephone calls and chilly reactions and being whispered about. The truth was that I had gotten used to it. I had learned how to answer curtly and not to allow friends and acquaintances and strangers to talk about Alenush. But Martha still hadn't gotten used to it. She had cut back on socializing and had even gradually stopped going to church on Sundays. The only person she saw almost every day was Danique.

Martha drank her coffee. She pulled a Kleenex from the box and wiped her eyes. Then she got up. "I'm going shopping. Will you be home for lunch?"

I looked at her. She had grown thinner over the past few years, and there were dark circles under her eyes. As she was leaving the room, she stopped and leaned against the wall, then turned around and looked at me. "I feel dizzy," she said, and smiled.

I was lining up the children at school one morning when the call came. I rushed to the hospital, and from then until the fortieth-day memorial for Martha – and for a long time afterward – life was a nightmare that just wouldn't end.

I am still looking at my cup of tea, which is no longer steaming. Danique is still talking. Some of her words I have heard, some not. She finishes with, "Instead of reassuring her that it wasn't her fault, you want to pour salt in the wound?" I raise my head.

My right leg has gone to sleep. Danique gets up, puts the untouched tea on the tray, and takes it back to the kitchen. I get up, go towards the table in the corner of the room and once again pick up Alenush's card. I open it. *Dear Aunt Dottie...* Her handwriting is just as it was when she was a child. The same uneven curves, illegible here and there, with no punctuation marks.

Alenush was in third grade when Martha started nagging her about her handwriting. "Isn't it shameful that the daughter of the school's principal writes so badly? What will people say?"

Alenush started to cry. "What did I ever do to deserve being the daughter of the principal? I wish I was Margar's daughter!" Margar was the school's janitor.

Danique puts a tray of fresh tea on the table. I spoon sugar into both of our cups.

When it's time to go, I push a few strands of white hair back from her forehead. I hold her hands for a few moments in my own, and say, "Thank you."

She raises her thin eyebrows and laughs. "For what?" She fixes my scarf, puts a little package in my hands, and says, "Happy Easter, Mr. Principal."

I open the box in the street. *What a fool! I didn't even take her any flowers.* I remember that I still need to buy a gift for Mohammad's wedding. In the little package there's a bottle of green ink, and I stand still for a few moments, smiling, then start walking again. "Tomorrow," I say aloud to myself. "Tomorrow I will buy Mohammad a gift."

The morning of the day after Easter, I sit at the dining-room table and look out at the garden. The violets lean this way and that in the breeze: it's as if they're finally at home in their new place.

On a piece of white paper, in green ink, I begin a letter: *Dearest Nunush…*

GLOSSARY

Places and proper names of people and foods that anglophone readers would not generally find familiar are identified in the text by an asterisk, and briefly explained below.

---

24 APRIL: this day is observed in Armenia, and by Armenians in diaspora, as Genocide Remembrance Day, and commemorates the victims of the Armenian genocide. On 24 April 1915, "Red Sunday," the Ottoman government in Istanbul rounded up and later executed some two to three hundred prominent members of the Armenian community (religious, political, and educational figures). Estimates of the number of Armenians killed in Ottoman territory during 1915–18 run anywhere from half a million to 1.5 million.

ALIK: an Armenian newspaper, founded in 1931, and published in Tehran. It is distributed throughout Iran.

ANAHITA: an old Persian word (*Nahid* in modern Persian) denoting an ancient Persian deity venerated as the goddess of the waters and associated with fertility, healing, and wisdom. Compared to the Semitic goddess Ishtar, Georges Dumezil has demonstrated that Anahita also corresponds to the Indian river goddess Saraswati. The second-century BCE Hellenic-style temple of Anahita at Kangavar (Iran) is one of the most important dedicated to this goddess. It is located halfway between Hamadan and Kermanshah. There is another well-preserved temple dedicated to Anahita in Bishapur near Kazeroon, south of Shiraz in the Fars province.

DOLMA: stuffed vine leaves (usually with rice, onions, and herbs). "Dolma" may also refer to other stuffed vegetables like sweet peppers or eggplants.

EJMIATSIN: formerly Vagharshapat (the name of the Arsacid king Vagharch I, 117–140). Ejmiatsin (also spelled Echmiadzin) is a town to the west of Yerevan in Armenia, home to the Mother Cathedral of Holy Ejmiatsin, a church built circa 303 CE that remains the central seat of the Armenian Apostolic Church and the Chief Catholicos of all Armenians, who is the chief bishop, or pope, of the Armenian Church. In

2000, this complex of religious buildings was listed as a UNESCO World Heritage site.

FEARLESS PILOT, THE: the name of a comic-book series that appeared for many years on the last page of *Children's World*, the *Junior Kayhan* newspaper.

GATA: a kind of Armenian puff pastry, round and about the size of a small plate. There are many varieties: some are made with a sweet filling, whereas others are unsweetened, or "salted." Sometimes, as with *paska*, we spread them with butter for breakfast.

GHORMEH SABZI: a Persian lamb-casserole dish made with kidney beans and sautéed mixed herbs such as fenugreek and parsley, served with rice. It is a popular dish in Iran, Iraq, and Azerbaijan, and is often said to be the Iranian national dish.

GILAKI: the Iranian dialect of northwestern Iran, in the Caspian province of Gilan.

IRIS: a type of confectionery like a marshmallow, square-shaped, about half the size of a matchbox. It is served wrapped in paper.

KAKACH: the Armenian word for tulip.

KARAJ: a town about twenty kilometers west of Tehran, in the foothills of the Alborz mountains. Today it is the fourth-largest city in Iran, and has become an extension of metropolitan Tehran. In the past, it was a popular resort for Tehranis, especially in the summer, with its large gardens and cooler climate.

KHORRAMABAD: an ancient city, the capital of Lorestan Province in southwest Iran, it is located in a scenic area on the road that goes up to Andimeshk Arak in the Zagros Mountains.

KUKU: a kind of thick omelet, rather like a Spanish omelet. It can be prepared with a variety of ingredients, for example, herbs (*sabzi*), potatoes, etc.

MOUNT ARARAT: Mount Ararat (Turkish *Ağrı*) is a snow-capped dormant volcano in Turkey (formerly West Armenia), formed of two peaks. The largest of the two is called Greater Ararat, or in Armenian, Grand Masis, which is the highest peak in Turkey standing at 5,137 m or 16,854 ft. The other, with an altitude of 3,896 m or 12,782 ft, is called Lesser Ararat, or in Armenian Petit Masis.

MUHARRAM: the first month in the Islamic (lunar) calendar, it is a month of remembrance or mourning.

NADERI (CAFÉ) / NADERI STREET: Naderi Street is one of the old streets in the historic center of Tehran. Located just north of the Grand Bazaar, many Armenians settled in this area in the last century. Café Naderi, opened in 1927, was the first European-style café in Tehran, and is a favorite meeting place for Armenians. Before the revolution of 1979, it was famous for its gardens and regular nightly entertainment. Throughout the twentieth century, it was a popular rendezvous for intellectuals and the middle-class residents of old Tehran.

NAZOUK: an Armenian rectangular butter pastry, close to the French *millefeuille*.

NIOC: the National Iranian Oil Company. Prior to 1951, when it was nationalized under Mossadegh, it was called the Anglo-Iranian Oil Company.

NOROUZ: the Persian New Year, a big national and largely secular holiday occurring at the Spring Equinox.

PASKA: a sweet Easter bread similar to the Italian *panettone*, flavored with orange zest. At Easter, you will typically find a *paska* on the table of Armenian families in Iran, the surface decorated with crosses and flowers.

QAVAM AL-SALTANEH: this street is located in central Tehran, perpendicular to Naderi Street. It is now called 30 Tir Street.

ST. THADDEUS MONASTERY: a famous Armenian monastery in Iran's western province of Azerbaijan, twenty kilometers from Maku. Armenians believe a church was originally built on this site in 66 CE, dedicated to the martyred apostle, St. Thaddeus (also called St. Jude), but it was extensively rebuilt in 1329. The earliest parts of the church were built of black stone, hence its Turkish name, the Black Church. In 2008 it was listed as a UNESCO World Heritage site.

SHERBET: a cold refreshing sweet drink made from fruit juice or fruit syrup, similar to lemonade, but made in various flavors, such as rose water, sour cherry, and plum.

SHOLEH ZARD: a popular Persian dessert of sweetened boiled rice flavored with saffron and rose water.

SULTAN HAMID II: Sultan Abdul Hamid II (1842–1918) was the ninety-ninth Caliph of Islam and the thirty-fourth Sultan of the Ottoman Empire, which he ruled from 1876 until his deposition by the Young Turk Revolution in 1909. He was the son of Abdul Mecid I and an Armenian member of the royal harem, named Tir-i Mujgan Kadin Efendi. He was replaced by one of his brothers, Mehmed V.

VIGEN: Derderian (1929–2003) was a very popular Iranian singer of Armenian background. After singing in pubs, he was spotted by Radio Tehran, and went on to introduce original pop songs along Western lines into the Persian language. He also starred in over thirty Iranian movies in the 1950s and 1960s. His tall good looks and his career as an actor and singer earned him the title of the Sultan of Pop, and "the Elvis Presley of Iran."